A tall man with a harsh, tanned face stood on the threshold.

"Mary," he said in a husky voice.

Before Emily could protest, the tall man had swept her into his arms, forced her chin up, and started punishing her mouth with a deep and savage kiss which held in it ten long years of frustrated passion.

It's the earl, thought Emily. He was supposed to come tomorrow. She became aware of strange surgings in her own body, a feverish heat swept over her, and then she forgot everything and everybody and kissed him back. . . .

Fawcett Crest Books
by Marion Chesney:

THOSE ENDEARING YOUNG CHARMS

Marion Chesney

FAWCETT CREST • NEW YORK

A Fawcett Crest Book
Published by Ballantine Books
Copyright © 1986 by Marion Chesney

Library of Congress Catalog Card Number: 85-91222

ISBN: 0-449-20533-9

Manufactured in the United States of America

First Edition: April 1986

For Max Brandt
with Love

Chapter One

Rain thudded down on the roof and chuckled in the lead gutters. Rain grew into small lakes in the middle of the lawn and turned the drive leading up to the front door of The Elms into a quagmire. Rain streamed down the misted windows of the drawing room and tumbled down the chimney in fat, sooty drops to spit on the fire.

"Will it *never* end," sighed Mary Anstey, putting down her sewing. "It has been raining for weeks and weeks."

"Only a week, Mary," said her sister, Emily. "You are worried that *he* will be kept away by the state of the roads."

"No, it is not that," said Mary slowly. "I think it is the weather that is making me feel so apprehensive. It has been ten years since I saw Captain Tracey. Ten years is a *very* long time. Now he is an earl. Just think! My Peregrine, the Earl of Devenham. Sometimes I'm frightened of meeting a stranger."

"He will be the same," said Emily stoutly. "You have waited for him all these years, as he has waited for you."

Mary gave a little sigh and picked up her sewing. She and Emily, despite the difference in their ages—Mary was twenty-nine and Emily, nineteen—were remarkably alike. Although Emily was a lively blond beauty, and Mary sedate and brownhaired, they could almost have passed for twins. The years did not seem to have touched Mary, thought Emily affectionately. Her face was still young and delicate and sweet.

Ten years ago Captain Peregrine Tracey had proposed to Mary Anstey, but her parents had refused to let her accept the hand of a penniless captain.

Mr. and Mrs. Anstey were kind, cheerful, and extremely vulgar. They had sprung from modest beginnings. Mr. Anstey had made his money in the City as a merchant and had retired to the country at an early age to enjoy his fortune and to remove himself from "the smell of the shop." He aspired to become a country gentleman, but failed to adapt to the country or to become a gentleman, since he was a pushy vulgar man. His wife supported him with equal vulgarity and insensitivity. Fortunately, their daughters had not inherited their coarseness but often found the many snubs their parents received from the local county very hard to take. They themselves had no friends, since they were not allowed to associate with the merchant class and were shunned by both gentry and aristocracy alike.

As long as Emily could remember, Mary had

lived for the arrival of the post. At first, Mrs. Anstey had confiscated all letters from Captain Tracey, but as the years went by and Mary remained a spinster, she was allowed to receive them.

Emily had been allowed to read a few of them. They all seemed rather cold and formal and, since Captain Tracey was serving in the peninsula, taken up with descriptions of the Spanish countryside. She secretly wondered at Mary's devotion to a man whom she, Emily, inwardly damned as a cold fish. She also wondered if Mary was aware that the vicar, the Reverend Peter Cummings, was madly in love with her.

When Mr. and Mrs. Anstey received the news that the despised captain had fallen heir to an earldom, their joy knew no bounds, and, of course, they themselves wrote to assure the new earl of a warm welcome.

He replied to them—not to Mary—saying he would be returning in November and would appreciate it if they would make immediate plans for the wedding.

It was a sharp lesson to young Emily in the ways of the world. All the county had accepted invitations to the wedding because Mary was to marry an earl. Emily did not see how her parents could bear to ask all the people who had snubbed them so unmercifully in the past, but Mr. and Mrs. Anstey were so triumphant at their daughter's social success that they seemed not even to trouble their heads with such petty considerations.

The earl was to arrive on the following day; the wedding was to be the following week. Emily found it hard to reconcile Mary's description of the shy young captain who had courted her ten years ago with the chilly, autocratic, formal letters that had arrived over the years. But then, everyone seemed to write very high-flown, stilted English.

Mrs. Anstey bustled into the room. She was a small, fat woman whose discontented face showed faint traces of the beauty she had had as a girl. She wore a starched muslin cap that stuck out at all angles, as if the laundress had given the cap a fright from which it had never recovered. Until the splendid news of the captain's elevation to the peerage, Mrs. Anstey had been inclined to bully her gentle older daughter, expressing loudly that it was a disgrace to have an old maid in the family, and God forbid that Emily should become an ape leader as well. Now her manner had changed to that of a fond and doting mama. She tiptoed around Mary the way one does around a sick person and addressed her in a meek whisper rather than in vulgar and strident tones.

On days like this, Emily longed to find out that she and Mary had been adopted and that they surely could not have come from such a parent. But she had only to glance up at the portrait of mama above the fireplace to see that Mrs. Anstey, painted as a young bride, had had all the beauty of both Mary and Emily before fat and discontent had ruined her features.

"At least we have nothing to be ashamed of," said Mrs. Anstey, plumping herself down on the sofa. "The earl will find everything here to be of the finest." She looked complacently round the drawing room as she spoke. Emily followed her gaze and sighed. Everything in their home was constantly

4

being changed. There were no comfortable old chairs, not one stick of furniture remaining from the days of her childhood. Only last spring, all the furniture had been taken out to the lawn and burned, including a pretty Hepplewhite escritoire of which Mary had been so fond.

Everything was now in the Egyptian mode, a fashion that had dominated the salons of London for some time and was now fast losing popularity. Emily reflected that what was not striped was sphinxed. Sphinxes' heads ornamented the tables and chairs and glass sphinxes' heads winked from the pilasters on the fireplace.

The Elms was a large, square box of a house, diligently kept free from any ivy or other creepers that might have softened the stark red of its brick outer walls. It was set back from the road which led out of the village of Malden Grand toward London. It had belonged to a Squire Haband, a man fondly remembered by the local county. The Ansteys had never met the squire, since he had died some months before Mr. Anstey purchased the house. Emily sometimes imagined him as a jolly and rubicund John Bull, not knowing that during his lifetime Squire Haband had been a rather nasty man and highly unpopular. He was only remembered fondly by the local county as a way of pointing out to the mushroom growth of Ansteys that they did not belong.

Mary was to be married in the local church. The Ansteys had been Nonconformist but had changed back to the established church on their arrival in the country, Mrs. Anstey insisting that the Church of England was more genteel.

Some of the young men of the county had been attracted by the beauty of the Anstey girls, not to mention their large dowries, but their parents had done all in their power to nip any budding romance. For the more Mr. and Mrs. Anstey craved social recognition, the more determined the local aristocracy and gentry became that they should not have it.

Until, of course, the announcement of Mary's forthcoming marriage to the Earl of Devenham.

Mr. Anstey came into the room and joined his wife on the sofa. He was as thin and spare as his wife was fat. He was dressed in what he considered to be the first stare. But his collar was too high and his waistcoat too short, and patches of pink scalp shone through his teased, frizzed, and pomaded hair.

"That's that," he said, rubbing his hands. "Hired two more footmen. His lordship shall not find us wanting in any of the comforts and elegancies of life."

Emily looked at her father curiously. "Will you not find it a trifle embarrassing, Papa, to face a gentleman whom you considered unsuitable when he first proposed to Mary?"

"No," said her father, all innocence. "Why should I? He *was* unsuitable then. He is not unsuitable *now*."

"Cannot one like people for their character rather than their rank, Papa?" pursued Emily.

Mr. Anstey wrinkled his brow and pondered the question. "No," he said at last. "No one does. 'Tain't the way of the world."

"Mr. Cummings does not think thus," said Mary

quietly. The Reverend Peter Cummings was the local vicar.

"Oh, that's his job," said Mrs. Anstey vaguely.

Emily felt she must escape. The furnishings were too new. Everything seemed to shout its newness and brashness at her. Even her mother's portrait had been recently "touched up." The huge looking glass on the wall facing the window doubled all the newness and glitter of the room.

Murmuring an excuse, she removed herself to the library at the back of the hall. But even this room looked as if the decorators had just packed up and left. Books bought by the yard from the bookseller shone in serried ranks of gold and calf behind the glittering plate glass of the new bookcases. New magazines with hard, shiny covers were neatly stacked on a hard, shiny table. Emily sat down on one of the new horsehair-stuffed chairs, leaned her chin on her hand, and thought hard.

At first, the return of Mary's beau had seemed very exciting. Like a romance come true. Had she not sighed with sentimental appreciation over the tales of how the great Duke of Wellinton had finally wed the love of his life, Kitty Packenham, so many years after his first offer of marriage had been turned down? Perhaps it was the incessant drumming of the rain that caused this sudden feeling of foreboding. Emily adored her elder sister, but she often felt that Mary was like a defenseless child in a harsh world. Sensitive to a fault, Mary often suffered deeply over the slights and snubs given to her parents. Emily herself felt better able to shrug them off, and she viewed local society with a cynical gaze.

Mary had certainly shown an unexpectedly stubborn turn of mind when she had repeatedly and resolutely refused a Season in London. The following April was to see Emily herself launched upon society, and *she* had not refused. She yearned to escape from home, and the only way for her to achieve that was to marry. Emily dreamed of setting up her own establishment under the indulgent eye of a suitable husband, and then sending for Mary to come live with them. Now, of course, that would not be necessary. Mary had promised in her gentle way to launch Emily into society. But before that blessed day arrived, Mary would be gone from The Elms, taking with her all her gentle companionship and leaving Emily to endure the long, boring, lonely days driving about the country with her mother.

Mrs. Anstey made calls on all the local notables, despite the fact that they were practically always "not at home." Emily would try to ignore the glances of pity and amusement exchanged by the footmen as the inevitable snub was delivered. The fact that after Mary's marriage they would probably be received everywhere did not excite her in the least. There was no one among the local county she wished to call friend. She felt she would never forgive them for their cruelty. For, much as she disliked her parents' parvenu manners, Emily nonetheless loved them dearly and imagined they suffered when, in fact, they did not mind very much at all.

They slavishly endured the laws of society as

meted out by their neighbors and were confident that the day would arrive when they would be accepted.

Then there was the vicar, Mr. Peter Cummings, to consider. He was obviously very much in love with Mary, a fact of which Mary did not seem in the least aware.

Emily became aware of a strange glow in the room. She turned and looked at the window.

The rain had stopped.

She walked over and raised the sash. Sweet, rain-scented air flowed into the room, bringing with it the fragrance of evergreen and damp leaves. A pale watery sun shone through the skeletal branches of the great oak by the hedge. The puddles on the lawn turned into lakes of molten gold.

Emily stretched, raising her arms above her head, and took a deep breath, waiting for the anxiety in the pit of her stomach to disappear.

But her dark, uneasy mood would not lighten like the day outside. She remembered the Earl of Devenham's chilly, formal letters.

Then her anxiety crystallized. She was afraid.

Emily Anstey was very much afraid that this earl returning from the wars would bear no resemblance to the shy young man who had stolen Mary's heart away.

The false spring gilding the November day had tempted Mary Anstey to leave the house. With a calash over her hat to protect her head in case the rain should return, and pattens on her feet to raise her above the mud, she walked rapidly in the direction of the village. Above the trees towered the spire of St. Martin's. Mary Anstey was seeking sanctuary from her troubled thoughts, hoping the peace and solitude of the church would take away the worries and anxieties that had come to plague her after the initial excitement of her forthcoming marriage had died down.

She walked around the church on a narrow, well-worn path and let herself in by a side door.

The church was still and empty, faintly scented with incense, charcoal, old paper, and damp hassocks. A few candles flickered in the cool, dim light, and a double column of arches soared up and vanished into the blackness at the roof.

Instead of entering the family pew, Mary sat down on a little rush-bottomed chair at the back of the church. She tried to let her mind float away from its worries, off into the dimness of the church, but all the little anxieties kept nagging at her brain.

I am old, she thought. Ten years older since he saw me last. I am practically an ape leader, yet he will be considered in his prime. I know his pride was deeply hurt by Papa's rejection of his suit. Oh, dear! I do remember Peregrine had a great deal of pride—brave and touching in a young man. But what if that pride has hardened into arrogance? I am so nervous I can hardly remember him. But I am very lucky, she chided herself. It is sinful to be so ungrateful. I am marrying the only man I have ever loved. Dear Emily will be able to come and live with us. . . .

A shadow crossed her face. She had always assumed Emily would always be with her. But what if her husband had other ideas?

She looked up with a start to find the vicar, Mr. Cummings, surveying her anxiously.

"I was thinking so hard," said Mary, rising to her feet and dropping him a curtsy, "that I did not hear your approach, Mr. Cummings."

"You look distressed," he said. "It must be a very worrying time for you."

"But I am very happy!" exclaimed Mary. "I am to finally marry the man of my choice."

Mr. Cummings's eyes were level with her own. Mary thought she had never before noticed how blue they were or how kind. He had a square, boyish face, although he was in his late thirties, and an unruly thatch of fair hair, which had a habit of sticking straight up from his head no matter how much he tried to water it down.

"I should think," said Mr. Cummings, turning his eyes away from Mary's face to stare at the traceried panels of the alms box, "that it must, however, cause some worry and concern to be seeing one's fiancé for the first time in ten years. But everything will be all right when you *do* see him."

"Do you *really* think so?" asked Mary, with a sudden rush of gratitude. "I *was* worried, and how very perceptive of you to guess. But you are quite right. It is the waiting and . . . and . . . wondering that make me nervous."

"It is a very fine thing to be marrying an earl," said Mr. Cummings, almost as if he were trying to convince himself. "One should not think of such worldly matters as rank and title, but at least you are not being forced into a distasteful marriage. That I do not think I could bear." The last sentence

11

was said in such a low voice that Mary did not hear it.

"Your parents are well, I trust?" added Mr. Cummings quickly. "And Miss Emily?"

"Oh, yes. We are all invited to the Harrisons for supper. Mama is in high alt."

"And you?"

"I think it is very gracious of Sir James and Lady Harrison," said Mary, primly.

"And yet," said Mr. Cummings, "I have seen Sir James and his lady snub your parents quite dreadfully outside this very church."

Mary sighed. "That was before I was known to be marrying an earl. For my part, I do not care to go, but you must realize it means so much to Mama."

Mr. Cummings looked at the delicate oval of Mary's face, at the brown curls peeping out from under the clumsy covering of her calash, at the faint shadows under her wide brown eyes. He seemed to be in the grip of some strong emotion. He half held out his hand toward her, and Mary saw with a kind of wonder that the hand shook slightly.

"Miss Anstey," he began. There was a silence. The wind rose and howled about the church. Up in the steeple, a bell moved and sent down a high, silvery chime. The candles on the altar flared and dipped and flared again.

"Yes, Mr. Cummings?" Mary studied his face anxiously, wondering if he was ill.

"I simply want to wish you all the happiness in the world," he said in a stifled voice. "I have some calls to make in the parish. Allow me to escort you home."

It was a very silent walk, Mr. Cummings wrapped in his own thoughts and Mary brooding once more on how she would feel about her fiancé when she saw him on the morrow.

Mary said good day to Mr. Cummings, and hurried up the short drive toward home, unaware that the vicar was still standing mournfully in the road, hat in hand, watching her until she was out of sight.

Miss Emily Anstey toyed with her food at the Harrison supper table and reflected that Sir James and his lady were amazingly like her own parents. They were loud, blunt, and crude. But Mr. and Mrs. Anstey had a certain warmth and kindness that was all too lacking in the Harrisons. Sir James had made it quite plain, over the turtle soup, that he was doing the Ansteys an immense favor by allowing them to cross his threshold. His wife asked innumerable questions about the earl, saying she quite doted on him already. Their son, Billy Harrison, a squat, rather brutish youth, was mercifully silent, although his parents, with many broad winks and hints, put out that he was quite enchanted with Miss Emily.

Emily's head began to ache and ache, until it seemed as if the pounding in her temples was drowning out every other sound in the room.

Then she heard Mary's voice. "You have become quite white, Emily. I fear you are unwell."

"It is the headache," said Emily wretchedly. "I feel if I could return home and lie down, I might recover quickly. I am sorry Sir James, Lady James, but I fear I must take my leave."

Mary volunteered to accompany her sister, but her move was pooh-poohed on all sides. The future countess was to be kept till the bitter end.

At last, it was decided that Emily should return alone and send the carriage and servants back again. Feeling a trifle guilty, Mrs. Anstey volunteered to accompany her daughter, but Emily, with the thought of escape so near, was quite vehement in her insistence that she would do very well alone.

As soon as she was safely ensconced in the darkness of the carriage, her headache disappeared like magic. Emily thought of Mary left to the tender mercies of the Harrisons and debated whether to return. But it would be considered very odd of her, and no doubt Sir James and Lady Harrison, whose vanity was only matched by their doting affection for their brutish son, would decide she had returned to be at repulsive Billy Harrison's side.

The Elms seemed like a sort of modern furniture shop to Emily as she stood in the hall, unfastening the strings of her bonnet after having sent the carriage back.

Everything was so quiet and polished and new and glittery and hushed. It would hardly have surprised her, she thought, if a deferential young man in a long-tailed coat had emerged from the shadows and tried to sell her the hall table. The only things lacking in the house were little white cards with prices on them.

She raised her hands to her head to remove her bonnet and then stood frowning, her hands still up to her head.

There was a bustle and commotion outside. Perhaps some of the neighbors had come to call, although the hour was late. The servants, apart from those who had returned to wait for the rest of the Anstey family, had been given the evening off.

Emily wondered whether to answer the door or pretend there was no one at home.

She hesitated, wondering what to do. The knocker resounded against the door. The imperative rapping seemed to make up her mind for her.

She swung the door open.

A tall man with a harsh, tanned face stood on the threshold. He was dressed in the first stare from his curly, brimmed beaver hat to his many-caped driving coat, opened to reveal a glimpse of formal dress, white cravat, and snowy linen.

"Mary," he said in a husky voice.

Before Emily could protest, the tall man had swept her into his arms, forced her chin up, and started punishing her mouth with a deep and savage kiss, which held in it ten long years of frustrated passion.

"It's the earl," thought Emily. "He was supposed to come tomorrow." She made a faint noise against the hardness of the lips pressing down on her own, but that only seemed to inflame the earl further. "I cannot possibly say anything until he is finished," thought Emily, resigning herself to his embrace.

That was a mistake. She became aware of strange surgings in her own body, a feverish heat swept over her, and then she forgot everything and everybody and kissed him back with such passion that the earl groaned in his throat and picked her up in his arms and carried her across the threshold. Her hat tumbled off onto the tiled floor of the hall. The soft glow from the latest thing in oil lamps shone on the gold of her hair.

"The deuce!" said the Earl of Devenham, releasing his grip. Emily fell with a crash onto the hall floor.

She sat up, rubbing her back, and looked ruefully up into the cold gray eyes of the earl.

"Welcome home, my lord," said Emily Anstey, overcome by an unmaidenly fit of giggles. "W-welcome h-home."

Chapter Two

The Earl of Devenham stood in front of the fireplace in the drawing room. He had divested himself of his coat, hat, and gloves.

He took out his quizzing glass and turned it this way and that in the light to make sure there was no mark on it, and then raised it to one eye and surveyed the slight figure of Emily Anstey.

Emily looked calmly back until he the glass let fall. He had not said a word since he had helped her to her feet in the hall.

"I owe you an apology," he said in chilly accents. "With the bonnet hiding your hair, I took you for Mary. You, I gather, are Emily. I remember you well. Always getting in the way." His level gaze seemed to imply that she had not changed.

"You did not allow me time for explanations," Emily said crossly. She remembered that kiss and tried to fight down the blush she could feel rising to her cheeks.

"You have not accepted my apology."

"Your apology is accepted." Emily bobbed a curtsy. "It is the servants' night off. Mary and mother and father are visiting a neighbor. I returned because I had the headache. I do not have it now. Would you care for some refreshment?"

A flash of humor briefly lit up his eyes as he listened to the staccato sentences and surveyed the stiff little lady before him. "I would like some wine," he said in more gentle tones.

"Of course." Emily hesitated in the doorway. "We expected you tomorrow, my lord."

"I was anxious to see my future bride," he said curtly. Then he smiled. "I fear you may have taken all the first warmth of my greeting. I had hoped to reserve it for Mary."

Emily opened her mouth to reply and found that she could not think of anything to say.

She turned and left the room. When she pushed open the door leading to the servants' dining room she found the staff seated at table.

The butler, Parsons, rose at her entrance, followed by the rest of the servants.

"I am so sorry, Parsons," said Emily. "Lord Devenham has arrived and wished wine and . . . and . . . perhaps he has not eaten. I did not think to ask. Mama said it was your evening off, so . . ."

"I will attend to it immediately, Miss Emily," said Parsons. "His lordship's room is ready for him."

"But it is your evening off. . . ."

"There is nowhere to go in Malden Grand," said Parsons. "Please return upstairs, Miss Emily. I will follow in a few moments to attend to Lord Devenham's wishes."

"There really *is* nothing to do," thought Emily, as she scurried back upstairs. "I never thought about it before. I imagined them all visiting other servants, but other servants never seem to have evenings off at all."

Emily realized with some surprise that her mother, despite her faults, was a kind mistress, and the thought gave her a comforting glow inside. The elegant and formidable earl, with his rich clothes and studied elegance, had been making her dread the return of her parents, so it was pleasant to think of something worthy about them. Certainly the earl must consider them harsh for having refused his suit. On the other hand, even a little place like Malden Grand was full of gossip about Miss This or Mr. That who had had their love life equally ruined. Meg, the baker's daughter, was in love with a farm laborer, Jim Smithers, but the baker considered Jim far beneath them, so the romance was not allowed to flourish. Because Mr. Anstey had worked hard and long to make his fortune, it was understandable in a way that he should want the best for his daughters when it came to marriage. Mr. Anstey was fond of saying that love and poverty could not live together.

Emily hesitated in the hall. She vaguely remembered the earl when he had been young Captain Tracey. Well, the young and eager captain had gone and was now this formidable amalgam of elegance and tailoring. What on earth would shy little Mary make of him now?

Taking a deep breath, Emily entered the drawing room. She was struck afresh by the harsh and handsome sophistication of the man facing her. His gray eyes were as cold as the North Sea and his jet black hair grew to a widow's peak on his forehead. He had an autocratic nose and thin, supercilious black brows. His face was tanned, his mouth hard and severe. His mouth . . . One would never think, looking at that hard and uncompromising mouth, that only a short time ago . . .

Emily blushed. "The servants are here . . . I m-mean, they did not go out, and Parsons, that's our butler, will be bringing your wine directly."

At that moment, Parsons entered behind Emily, bearing a tray with a decanter of wine and one of brandy which he set on a table beside the fire.

In a stately way, he welcomed the earl to The Elms, and in a cold, businesslike way, the earl rapped out instructions as to the housing of his servants, the care of his baggage, and the grooming of his horses.

Parsons expanded under these curt instructions. This was just the sort of behavior he expected from one of the quality, and since he was fond of his master and mistress, the butler was gleefully looking forward to seeing this high and mighty lord snubbing the local gentry in the same way as Mr. and Mrs. Anstey had been snubbed.

As Parsons was bowing himself out—backward, as if retreating from the presence of royalty—Emily said, "Oh, do send someone over to Sir James's, Parsons, and tell my parents that my lord is arrived."

When Parsons had left, Emily sat down gingerly

on the edge of a chair and surveyed her future brother-in-law with some trepidation.

Embarrassed into saying the first thing that came into her head, she blurted out, "You are not as I remember you."

He poured himself a glass of wine and said over his shoulder, "You will take wine with me?" He poured a glass for Emily without waiting for her reply.

"You are not as I remember you, either, Miss Emily," he said, turning and handing her a brimming glass. "You are remarkably like your sister. That is what deceived me. I did not know it was you until I saw the color of your hair. It was always golden."

"Mary is still the same," said Emily. She took a great gulp of wine, choked slightly, and rubbed her nose, hoping she would not sneeze. "People often think we are twins."

"I am glad time has stood still for Miss Anstey," said the earl coldly. A bitter look crossed his face. "I cannot say the same for myself."

"No," said Emily naively, "now, you look like an earl."

"Indeed? The few earls of my acquaintance are portly and elderly. I did not know an earl looked like anything in particular."

"Well, you know, my . . . my lord . . ."

"You may call me Peregrine."

"Thank you. I mean you look so cold and haughty," said Emily earnestly. "Just like a character in a book I'm reading."

"Which book?"

"The Travels of Lord Sapphire."

21

"And I look like this Lord Sapphire?"

"No, my . . . Peregrine. But there is this marvelous villain called the Earl of Perrengo, and he is most harsh and wicked. The heroine, the Lady Bianca, repulses his advances, but he is very lustful, you see," went on Emily, so enthralled in the story that she quite forgot the earl was in the room. "Lord Sapphire is quiet and noble. Of course, he is not a lord at the beginning of the book, for his wicked nurse put her daughter's baby in the cradle and sent *him* out to be brought up by lowly woodcutters. He rescues Bianca just as the earl is carrying her off to his castle in the mountains."

"Does he throw her over his saddlebow?"

"Yes!" said Emily, delighted and surprised. "How *did* you guess?"

"Oh, I do it all the time."

"It was a monstrous exciting story," said Emily, clasping her hands in her lap. "Lord Sapphire was so good and noble, and Mary said he was a splendid sort of man, but I rather thought the villain the more exciting. You see . . ."

"I have never heard such a farrago of nonsense in all my life," said the earl.

"How sad. I suppose you are one of those people who think novels wicked and only read improving books."

"Exactly."

Emily took another gulp of her wine. If only Mary would come home!

After a long silence, Emily ventured, "You know, since you find the tone of my conversation too low, it might be civil of you to suggest a topic."

"Perhaps," he said moodily. He turned and

kicked a log in the fire with one Hessian-booted foot. Unfortunately, the log contained a great amount of hot resin; the resin stuck to his boot and the boot caught fire.

"Get your boot off! Get your boot off!" screamed Emily.

"I *am* getting it off," he said testily. "No, don't . . ."

But he was too late.

Emily had snatched up the decanter of brandy and poured it over his smoking boot, which burst into blue and yellow flames.

"Idiot!" howled the earl.

He raced out of the room, out of the hall, out of the house, with Emily hard at his heels.

"Please return to the house, Emily," the earl said crossly, as he stood with one foot steaming in a puddle on the lawn. "It has started to rain."

"I didn't know brandy burned!" wailed Emily, wringing her hands. "I shall never drink it. Never! Only think of the damage to one's internal being."

"I really don't think the damage is at all the same," said the earl, limping back toward the house, "unless you drink a glass of brandy and throw a lucifer down after it."

He sat in a chair in the hall and ruefully examined the charred remains of his boot. "Another pair of boots, John," he said without raising his voice.

"Very good, my lord," came a voice from the landing above, and Emily started.

"My Swiss," explained the earl. "He is invaluable. Always somewhere on hand."

"I am truly sorry about your boot," said Emily earnestly.

He watched her expressive little face with some interest. A deep and dark thought had obviously just struck her.

"Perhaps God was punishing you because you were so haughty about my taste in novels," said Emily slowly. "Pride cometh before a fall, and a haughty heart . . . How does it go?"

"My dear child, if you are going to go about seeing the hand of the Almighty in every trivial domestic accident, you will end up in Bedlam. You are not a Methodist, I trust?"

"Oh, no, my . . . Peregrine. We were Nonconformist, Papa says, but Mama said it was not a genteel religion. I should not have told you that," added Emily miserably. "I feel a great weight on me at the moment, you see, what with you kissing me because you thought I was Mary and no one else being here."

"You will not be alone much longer," remarked the earl. "I hear a carriage arriving."

His servant put a new pair of glossy Hessians on the earl's feet.

"It is wonderful that your foot was not burned," said Emily, hoping to put him in a good mood so that Mary would not receive too much of a shock.

But the earl had risen to his feet and was watching the doorway. There was an intensity about him, a stillness, a waiting. Emily felt an odd little pang of envy and wondered if any man would ever wait for her in such a way.

The door opened; Parsons materialized to take cloaks and hats. Mr. and Mrs. Anstey came rushing forward, babbling welcomes, my lords, and apologies.

The earl hardly seemed to hear them. He was looking across their heads to where Mary stood, just inside the door. Mary's eyes had lit up in welcome, but gradually the glow left her face and she looked wary and frightened.

Then the earl turned slowly and looked at Emily, a little crease between his brows.

"If only he would kiss her as he kissed me," thought Emily. "If only he would say *Mary* with that special husky note in his voice."

But the earl walked forward and formally raised Mary's hand to his lips.

"I am glad to see you, Mary," he said. "It has been a long time."

"Very long," whispered Mary.

Mary raised her eyes, and Emily, who knew her so well, read the unspoken words in her wide, frightened gaze. *Too long.*

Chapter Three

Two days had passed since the arrival of the earl.
Emily did not know what Mary was really thinking about. There seemed no time now to sit and
chat. The house was in an uproar, with guests beginning to arrive, caterers discussing catering,
musicians discussing music, and Mr. Parsons hir-
ing extra staff.

The weather was cold and clear. Two large mar-
quees were to be erected on the lawn at the back of
the house, one for dancing and the other for food.

It came to be known that the Earl of Devenham
was not pleased that accommodation had not been
arranged for relatives from his side of the family.
Mr. Anstey had naively thought that since the
earl's parents were dead, it followed that he did not
have any relatives at all.

The local inn had to be taken over and rooms
found in various private houses for the other remaining guests. Society was quite prepared to

house the earl's relatives. No one really wanted the Anstey relatives, whom they damned as being either pushing and vulgar or faded and vulgar.

Emily knew that the day after his arrival, the earl had taken Mary out for a drive. When they had returned, Mary had looked quiet and resigned, and the earl more taciturn than ever. One thing was certain. They were no longer in love.

But there was no sign of either of them calling off the wedding, thought Emily miserably. Mary seemed determined to put a brave front on things and kept saying in her quiet way that she was very happy.

Emily twisted one golden curl nervously around one finger and looked out of the drawing room window to where Mary could be seen hurrying down the drive.

She is going to the church, thought Emily. I do hope she does not find our poor Mr. Cummings is in love with her. It would be just too much to bear. Mary is too sweet, too retiring, for such a cold autocrat as Devenham. If only there were something I could *do*!

Suddenly it all seemed very silly to Emily that two people should get married just because they felt they had to. Mary was a dutiful girl, but surely the earl could be appealed to. He possessed a great fortune. It should be easy for him to find a bride.

Emily decided to try to speak to him before her courage failed her.

She knew he had gone to The Green Man, the inn in Malden Grand, to meet his friend, Arthur Chester, who was to be bridesman. She would slip out of the house and ride into the village. If Mama caught her, she could say she had to buy ribbons for her gown.

Emily took a great deal of time over her appearance, putting her unusual concern over the niceties of her dress down to nerves. At last, attired in a fashionable riding habit of bright green cloth, ornamented down the front and on the cuffs with black braid *à la Militaire*, a small riding hat of black beaver trimmed with a gold cordon and tassels, and a long green ostrich feather and black half-boots, laced and fringed with green, Emily rode off on her little gray mare, Sylvia.

For a little of the way, she simply enjoyed the ride; she had been pent up in the house for an unconscionable period of time because of the long days of rain.

It was only as she was approaching the inn that Emily's courage began to desert her. Papa would learn she had ridden out without a groom and would give her a lecture, and God forbid he should find out the nature of her visit. What if Lord Devenham had told him! Somehow, Emily could never think of the austere earl as Peregrine.

But the thought of Mary's sad, sweet, resigned face drove her on.

The inn seemed to be full of people coming and going. The earl may once have been plain Captain Peregrine Tracy, but that did not preclude his having a great many very grand relatives. They were distinguishable from the other guests at the inn by seeming to be very tall, very hard-faced, and very haughty.

As Emily went in search of the landlord, one lady

who appeared to be all nose and glaring eyes said in a loud voice to her companion, "Well, if dear Peregrine is set on tying himself down to a family of counterjumpers, there is nothing we can do."

The landlord informed Miss Emily Anstey that the Earl of Devenham was abovestairs in Mr. Chester's private parlor. He would ask my lord to descend to the coffee room.

Heart beating hard, Emily selected a quiet and dark corner and sat waiting, pressing her knees together to try to stop their trembling.

When the earl entered the room, stooping to pass through the low doorway, Emily's courage nearly deserted her. His face wore a closed and shuttered look as he approached her. He looked not in the least pleased to see her.

"I had hoped it was my fiancée," he said abruptly. "Is anything the matter?"

"No, Devenham," said Emily, deciding Devenham was a compromise between Peregrine and my lord.

"Then it was you who were overcome by an irresistable desire to see me?"

"No, Devenham."

"Well, Miss Emily, and what is you pleasure?"

The drawled words held a mocking note.

Emily raised her eyes to his and took a deep breath. "I have come," she said, "to talk to you about your forthcoming marriage."

"Odso! And . . . ?"

"And after careful observation, I have decided that Mary and you are not in love with each other."

"Mary has told you this?"

"Oh, no. Mary would not dream . . . Mary is so dutiful. . . ."

"Miss Emily," said the earl coldly, "I suggest you return home before I put you over my knee and smack you. Your sister is a woman of mature years and knows her mind. When a lady has waited faithfully for me for ten whole years, then it is my duty to marry her. Duty is a higher virtue than love. I suggest you keep you maudlin thoughts for those romances you read."

Emily flushed. She felt very young and silly.

"I am sorry," she whispered. "I love Mary and do not wish her to be unhappy." Emily hung her head.

He put out a long finger and tilted her chin up, noticing the glint of tears in her brown eyes.

"You are a mere child," he said in a gentle voice, "and yet a child with a tremendous power to make me angry. Get home with you, Miss Emily."

She stared into his eyes, seeing something there she did not understand, wondering what it was. His gaze seemed twined and joined with hers like the poet's thread. Color came into her face and her bosom rose and fell as she felt her breathing become restricted.

He released her chin, stood up, and, without another word, turned and stalked out of the coffee room.

Emily sat for a long time in silence. Never before had she felt so young and immature. In her humiliation, she began to think she had read signs of unhappiness into Mary's demeanor that did not really exist.

With a little sigh that was half a sob, she got to her feet. She felt as if she had left a very dashing and mondaine Miss Emily Anstey behind. It was a chastened schoolgirl who mounted her horse and rode away.

Mary Anstey sat in the quiet of the church and prayed desperately for faith, strength, and hope to go through with her marriage. After a time, she became aware of someone kneeling beside her. She tried to concentrate on her prayers, but she was plagued with the ridiculous idea that the person beside her could read her thoughts.

She rose to her feet.

"Miss Anstey."

Her silent companion in prayer had been Mr. Cummings.

"Mr. Cummings. It is a fine day, is it not? Our guests are seeing the countryside at its best."

"Yes," said Mr Cummings brightly, thinking of the bare, muddy fields outside and the skeletal branches of the winter trees.

"There is so much confusion and turmoil at home with all the preparations for the wedding," Mary rushed on, "that I felt I had to come here for some peace."

"And help?"

"Yes, naturally. One is always in need of spiritual guidance, no matter how . . . h-how h-happy one is." And with that, Mary sat down again and burst into tears.

"Please, don't," begged Mr. Cummings, running his hands through his stiff hair so that it stood up in spikes. "I cannot bear to see you in such distress. I know. You are worried about the wedding. Young brides are often so."

Mary dried her eyes very carefully and said in a flat little voice, "I don't love him. He frightens me."

"Ah!" Mr. Cummings let out a long breath and sat down beside her.

"He is not the man I knew," Mary went on. "He has changed. He is hard and cold. He frightens me."

"My dear Miss Anstey! The wedding must be called off. You must not go through with it."

"Yes, I must. I have a duty to my parents. This marriage means so much to them. So very much. I know they seem worldly and silly, but they are very kind."

"They were not very kind when they did not allow you to marry Devenham in the first place."

"They thought they were doing the best thing," Mary said wretchedly. One large tear rolled down her cheek and clung to a glossy brown curl, where it hung and shimmered in the candlelight of the church.

"I was very young. They thought I did not know my mind. And, oh, they were right! I have lived on dreams. He was so young and eager and unsure of himself when he was Captain Tracey, so gentle and kind. Now he is hard and demanding and overbearing."

"You are become quite white," said Mr. Cummings. "Let us walk in the churchyard a little. The fresh air will make you feel better."

"I do not think anything will make me feel better," sighed Mary, but she allowed him to lead her out of the church and into the hard wind and glitter of the day outside.

They walked around the back of the church to

where the tall, silent tombstones stood silhouetted against the pale blue sky.

"I do not know what to say to comfort you, Miss Anstey," said Mr. Cummings. He leaned one square, dependable hand against a dropsical-looking marble cherub with a face of ageless evil. "Any man would wish to marry you." He struck the cherub with his fist. "*Any* man. If I had the right. . . . but I must not say more. I should have spoken before this, but it all seemed hopeless. I knew you were waiting for him—waiting and longing—as I, too, have waited and longed."

Mary turned and looked at him, pity and amazement in her tear-washed eyes.

"I did not know, Mr. Cummings, that there was some young lady who. . . ."

Her voice died away before the blaze of love in his eyes.

For a long moment they stood looking at each other, Mr. Cummings with hopeless love and Mary with a dawning awareness of that love.

Wonderingly she raised a hand to his cheek and he grasped it, and, turning it over, pressed a kiss into the palm.

"There," he said in a ragged voice. "My secret is out. A fine man of God I am, Miss Anstey. Instead of lightening your burden, I am adding to it."

"Oh, no," said Mary sadly. "I did not know. But I know now, and it is a knowledge I will treasure always."

She turned and walked away around the side of the church.

There was nothing Peter Cummings could do but watch her disappear and think of the nightmare before him. In a few days' time he would be marrying the love of his life to another man.

The wedding rehearsal took place the following day. The bride-to-be was wan and shaken. The groom-to-be was curt to the point of rudeness, and snarled his responses. Emily Anstey was worried to death.

To her, it seemed glaringly plain that somehow or other Mr. Cummings had declared his love, and gentle Mary in her turn had fallen head over heels in love with the vicar.

"Of course, only I can know that," thought Emily. "Mary is so ill-looking, everyone else must surely think she has bride-nerves. Oh, dear, I must do something to stop this wedding. I don't care if Devenham is humiliated again. He *deserves* to be humiliated, the great, arrogant brute! See how he glares at poor Mary."

It was a relief when the rehearsal was over and the Earl of Devenham curtly refused an invitation to supper, saying he had matters to discuss with Arthur Chester.

"What's amiss?" Mr. Arthur Chester asked curiously, once he and the earl were seated in the inn over a bowl of steaming punch. "You are in a nasty mood."

"She don't want me," said the earl abruptly.

"Then don't have her!"

"Oh, she'll get used to me in time. One woman is much like t'other. But I refuse to be turned down again by the Ansteys—and all because their henwitted daughter has fallen in love with the vicar."

"My dear boy!"

"I am not blind, you know."

"Then call it off!"

"No," said the earl stubbornly. "I loved that girl with all my heart and I shall come to love her again. And she, me! When the Ansteys with their monumental vulgarity told me ten years ago that I was not good enough for their daughter, I longed to make them eat their words. I longed to return in triumph and have them crawl at my feet."

"How gothic! Well, you have returned and nobody could crawl more. Leave her waiting at the altar. That way you will humiliate them the more, she can marry her vicar, and everything will be right and tight."

The earl looked at his friend's thin, dark, mobile face with great irritation.

"You make it all sound so easy. Just up and run. I have my pride. I have sworn to marry the girl, and marry her I will."

Mr. Chester twisted his neck uncomfortably. He was wearing the latest thing in high stiff collars—called patricides—and wished his laundress had not been quite so generous with the starch.

He was in fact Colonel Chester, late of the 10th Dragoons, but since he had retired from the army, he had dropped his military title and had sworn he did not even want to see a uniform again.

He was small in stature, with olive skin and a great beak of a nose. He was of a romantic turn of mind and had eagerly traveled to Malden Grand to see his friend marry the girl he had waited for for so long. He was disappointed to find this particular romance on the verge of such an unhappy ending.

"Well, don't you see," he ventured cautiously,

"she's a pretty little thing and very shy. You're so used to ordering men around and fighting battles, well, no one could say you've got a gentle touch with the fair sex. Pity you wasn't marrying the younger gel. Lots of fire there."

"Miss Emily Anstey is a minx," said the earl coldly. "I like my ladies to behave like ladies. Do you know she had the temerity to waylay me at this inn and tell me that neither I nor her sister was in love."

"Can't say I blame her for that. She had the right of it."

The earl poured himself a glass of punch. He suddenly remembered his arrival at The Elms. For a few brief, glorious moments, his return had been all he had ever dreamed it would be. *That* was what he had dreamed of all these long years. Not revenge. Warm lips, pliant body, surging senses.

When he had taken Mary for a drive, he had reined in his horses and taken her in his arms to kiss her. She had trembled at his touch, and her lips had been very cold, and her whole body had seemed to shrink from him. Damn that minx, Emily. Had it not been for the warmth of *her* response, Mary's withdrawal would have seemed the natural response of a virginal lady.

"She's a doxy!" he said savagely.

"Not Miss Anstey!"

"Never mind. It was someone else. The wedding is tomorrow. The guests are all here, and I'll just have to go through with it."

"You can't go through with it!" Emily Anstey said passionately, on the eve of the wedding.

Her sister raised a tear-stained face from the pillow. "I must."

"He doesn't love you," said Emily firmly. "Mr. Cummings does."

"Oh, don't. Oh, that I had never known. Go away, Emily."

"Listen!" said Emily urgently, edging closer to her sister on the bed. "Do you remember two years ago when we played that trick? I put on a brown wig, and you a blond one. We went to the assembly as each other. We fooled everyone, even Mama and Papa! I will go tomorrow as you, and you will go as me. He will marry the wrong sister, and since I will make my vows as *Mary* Anstey, the marriage will not be legal, and he will be so shocked he will go away and never see us again. I read such a thing in *Lady Jane's Dilemma*. She was to marry. . . ."

Mary sat up in bed and stared wide-eyed at her sister. "I have never heard of such a *criminal* idea," she gasped. "Peregrine would *shoot* me. Now, leave me alone this instant and don't let me hear you talk such fustian again. No! Not another word."

Emily went to her own room and sat in a chair by the window, watching the patterns the rushlight made on the ceiling.

Somehow the marriage must be stopped. Now just suppose she, Emily, managed to drug Mary. While Mary slept, she could put the blond wig on her head and go downstairs in the brown wig, pretend to be Mary, and say that Emily was so ill she could not attend the wedding. That dim, myopic cousin, Bertha, would be delighted to be elected bridesmaid.

The earl would be furious with her, would take

out his wrath on her, but he would not blame Mary. So Mary could then marry Mr. Cummings, because after the disgrace, papa would let Mary marry *anybody*. Thank goodness no one had heard of her visit to the earl at The Green Man.

Emily began to plot and plan. It was no use drugging Mary now. She might have slept off the effects by the morning. Better to take her her morning chocolate. Emily groaned. She found it very hard to wake up early even at the best of times.

"Then you will just have to sit up all night, miss," Emily told herself severely. "By morning, you will look every bit as wan and pale as Mary."

A picture of the earl's furious, arrogant face rose before Emily's eyes, and she shuddered. But Mary must be saved at all costs. Mary had suffered enough and should suffer no more.

Setting her lips in a stubborn line, Emily lit the candles, picked up a romance, and prepared to wait out the night.

It was a blessing that the Anstey sisters' lady's maid was new to the job. Their former lady's maid had recently retired with a good pension. The current one, Felice, a black-eyed French girl whose sole interest in life seemed to be the second footman, dressed her charges in an efficient but impersonal way, and, Emily was sure, had never studied them closely enough to tell them apart.

Emily had drugged Mary's morning chocolate with laudanum, placed the blonde wig on her sister's head, and drawn the covers up about her face.

Attired in the brown wig and with her lively features carefully schooled to copy Mary's demure expression, Emily was sure that with the help of the thick white veil which went with the wedding dress, she could easily pass for her sister.

As soon as Mary had drunk the drugged chocolate and gone back to sleep, Emily told Felice to inform Mama that "Emily" was too ill to attend and to take the bridesmaid's gown to Cousin Bertha with the plea that Bertha perform Emily's part during the service.

Although it was not yet time to get dressed, Emily then urged Felice to help her into the white silk wedding gown, trimmed with seed pearls and Valencienne lace, so that she was gowned and veiled by the time Mrs. Anstey came upstairs to look at poor "Emily" and wonder what Emily was doing sleeping in Mary's room.

Emily gave her mother a long tale of nighttime headaches and sickness and said that "Emily" had begged to be allowed to rest and would join the family at the wedding celebrations.

Mrs. Anstey tiptoed into Mary's room and gazed down anxiously at the sleeping figure on the bed, while Emily fretted, hoping that her mother would not draw back the covers and guess that the girl in bed was not Emily.

The enormity of what she was about to do did not really strike Emily. She set her sister's happiness far above the haughty earl's humiliation and far above any embarrassment to the Anstey family.

She was also living in a dream world, playing out the part of a heroine in a novel. In fact, when all was discovered, Emily planned to faint, quite in the best manner, because surely no one would rant and curse an unconscious girl.

She prayed and prayed that her mother would stay away until the time came to set out for the church, but Mrs. Anstey considered it her duty to hint delicately at the mysteries of the marriage bed. Fortunately, this caused the good lady so much anguish and embarrassment that she looked anywhere in the room but at Emily.

All at once it was time to leave. Flushed with excitement at appearing in the limelight for once in her life, Cousin Bertha looked feverish and animated, her long nose pink with excitement. Her gown was rather full in the bust for her flat figure, but she had solved that problem by stuffing her reticule down the front.

As Emily stood at the entrance to the church, leaning on her father's arm, she suddenly felt sick with dread. As she looked at the glowing pride on her father's face, her conscience gave her such a sharp stab that she nearly cried aloud.

But, somehow, it was too late to turn back. The church door was open, the organ was playing, and her father began to lead her forward.

She approached the altar with her head meekly bowed, wishing her veil were thicker.

Then she raised her eyes and saw the earl standing stiffly at attention, watching her approach. He was wearing a rose silk coat so beautifully tailored that it seemed molded across his shoulders.

His knee breeches were of white silk and his shoes had diamond buckles. Diamonds blazed among the snowy folds of his cravat and on the buttons of his long silver-and-white waistcoat. His black hair was curled and pomaded and seemed to shine with blue lights in the dimness of the church.

Very stiff and white in his green and gold robes stood the vicar, Mr. Peter Cummings. He looked down to say a silent good-bye to his love and his gaze seemed to burn right through the white veil, as the sharp and anguished eyes of love detected the face of Miss Emily Anstey.

There was a long silence. The congregation began to fidget, wondering why the vicar did not begin.

Mr. Cummings drew a long, silent breath of relief. Obviously, Mary had found the courage at the last minute to say she would not wed the earl, and the earl had been content to take the younger sister instead.

Emily only realized what was happening when she heard the vicar say in measured tones, "Will you, Emily Martha Patterson Anstey, take this man to be your lawful wedded husband?"

Automatically she replied, "I will," and then she waited for the earl to shout that it was all a trick.

But he said nothing.

Stunned and shocked, Emily stood as if turned to stone as the lengthy wedding ceremony went on and on. As in a dream, she made the responses which she knew by heart, having attended many weddings, and also because she said them into her pillow to her dream lover on many spring nights.

She heard the earl promise to worship her with his body and endow her with his worldly goods.

Mr. Cummings' voice grew in strength. Triumphantly, he headed toward the end of the service.

"O Merciful Lord and Heavenly Father, by whose gracious gift mankind is increased, we beseech thee, assist with thy blessing these two persons, that they may both be fruitful in procreation of children, and also live together in godly love and honesty. . . ."

Children! thought Emily, feeling sick and faint.

Her head burned. The vicar's voice seemed to ebb and flow.

At last it was all over. She threw back her veil, helped clumsily by the over eager Cousin Bertha. The earl's eyes blazed down into her own. "Welcome, wife," he muttered between his teeth. I'm married to him, thought Emily weakly. Oh, what have I done?

Chapter Four

The scene in the vestry was dreadful. The parish register was open, awaiting the signature of the happy pair. Mr. Cummings was beaming all over his face, perfectly sure that nothing was amiss, only willing to believe the best.

Then it finally dawned on him that the earl was so cold and chilly he looked iced, and that Emily was wearing a brown wig and looked so white she seemed about to faint.

Mr. and Mrs. Anstey were standing proudly by, their faces lit up with happiness.

As far as they were concerned, it was Mary who stood before them.

"What's amiss, Mary?" demanded Mrs. Anstey cheerfully. "You are supposed to sign your name."

"I am not . . ." Emily began, swaying slightly as she stood, one hand on the book for support.

In a split second, it dawned on the reverend what had really happened and why Emily was wearing a brown wig. It was horrible! The scandal! And where was Mary?

He leaped into action. He murmured to Cousin Bertha and Mr. Chester that it was customary in St. Martin's for the married couples' attendants to wait in the main body of the church with the other guests. He prayed they would not protest.

To his relief, they left.

With a sinking heart, he looked up at the earl's face.

"Perhaps you would care to explain, Lord Devenham?"

The earl removed a snuffbox from his pocket and carefully took a delicate pinch. With maddening slowness, he returned the box to his pocket.

"What is going on?" demanded Mr. Anstey.

Summoning up all her strength, Emily willed herself not to faint. She raised shaking hands to her headdress and veil, removed both, and set them down on a vestry chair. Then, with one quick movement, she removed her wig. Her blond curls tumbled about her face.

"*Emily!*" cried Mr. and Mrs. Anstey.

"I'm sorry," said Emily. "So very sorry. But Mary was miserable. I thought if I took her place and it was discovered afterward to be me, then the marriage would not be a marriage at all."

"But you *are* married," said Mr. Cummings. "I recognized you, so I spoke your proper name."

The earl continued to stand cold and unblinking, his gray eyes fastened on Emily's face.

Mrs. Anstey raised chubby hands to her crumpled fat face. "The shame of it," she said, beginning to cry. "The humiliation. To have played such a trick. To have ruined our moment of glory. We shall be the laughing stock of the county."

Then Mr. Anstey began to berate his daughter, while Mr. Cummings kept demanding to know what had happened to Mary, and Mrs. Anstey bawled at full force.

In the midst of her misery and shame, Emily suddenly caught a faint gleam of humor in the earl's eyes. He had had his revenge on the Anstey family at last. And she had been the one who had got it for him.

Her noble gesture would appear to be a vulgar, hoydenish trick. The entire county would say she was jealous of Mary and wanted the earl for herself and so had drugged her sister's chocolate. Emily began to doubt her own sanity.

The Earl of Devenham felt a weary distaste for the whole business. He realized he did not love Mary Anstey. He felt quite sure it was highly unlikely he would ever repeat that folly of his youth by falling in love with anybody else.

For a moment, he had enjoyed the humiliation of the Ansteys. But as he looked at Mrs. Anstey's crumpled and pathetic figure, he saw a kindly, silly woman who had tried to do the best for her daughter.

He, Devenham, would have to marry to secure the line. He wanted children.

If he accepted the marriage, then he would be spared the tedium of a London Season with its attendant miseries of courtship. Emily was young and beautiful. She was wayward and childish, but she had acted with a certain gallantry.

His cool voice broke into a babble.

"I think the best thing to do," he said, "is to let the marriage stand."

It was then that Emily did faint.

Fortunately, she was caught by the earl before she hit the floor.

Mary Anstey struggled awake. Her head felt hot and heavy, and her mouth dry. Somewhere at the edge of her consciousness loomed a great black cloud of dread. She murmured sleepily and turned her face into the pillow, determined to go back to sleep.

And then it struck her.

This was her wedding day!

She glanced at the clock ticking busily on the mantel. Two in the afternoon.

No, it couldn't be that. The clock must be wrong. Her head was so hot. She put a hand up to her brow. Her nightcap felt so heavy. She felt under her chin to untie the strings and then frowned. She wasn't wearing a nightcap. Then what . . . ?

A wig!

She tugged it off and looked at the blond curls lying on the coverlet. She could almost hear Emily's voice whispering that ridiculous suggestion.

Mary tugged furiously at the bell rope and then waited. But no one answered. Her first thought was, of course, all the servants are at the wedding.

Her second—Emily's done it. She's masqueraded as me. She *must* not.

Mary leaped from bed and made a hasty toilet. Her legs felt weak, and she had a dreadful thirst.

Then she heard the sound of the village band and ran to the window and looked out.

In true country tradition, the wedding procession was walking back from the church to the house. Headed by the band, the Earl of Devenham and Emily led the procession. Even from this distance, Mary noticed that Emily was very white, although she was attempting to laugh at something the earl said.

Mary sank down in a chair, her head throbbing. It seemed as if the haughty earl—for she could hardly think of him as Peregrine now—had decided to go along with the joke. The guests all seemed in high spirits as well. Emily could not be married to the earl because she would take her vows as Mary Anstey.

The noise of the band drew nearer. There was the clink of glasses and dishes from the refreshment marquee on the lawn.

Mary wondered how she could possibly have overslept. She looked thoughtfully at her empty chocolate cup beside the bed. She picked it up and sniffed at it. Laudanum. She remembered Emily bending over her, urging her to drink it all up.

Mary felt that Emily had made too great a sacrifice. The Earl of Devenham was no longer the shy young captain she, Mary, had loved. He was a hardened, sophisticated, experienced man. Emily was little more than a schoolgirl. The isolated life the two sisters had led had seemed to stop Emily from maturing as other girls of her age.

It was her, Mary's, duty to go downstairs and help Emily face the music. If the other guests did not know the marriage was a fake, then they soon would.

At least, Emily had not paid the ultimate sacrifice of actually marrying the earl, thought Mary. She was sure Devenham was putting a face on things for the moment, but his pride and his temper would surely make him start to tongue-lash Emily any moment now.

She put her finest silk gown on over her petticoat and added a little rouge to her pale cheeks. She placed a smart velvet bonnet on her head and picked up her reticule. Mary squared her shoulders.

The first person she met, bustling up the stairs at a great rate, was her mother.

"Mary!" she gasped. "Was there ever such a thing! I would not have believed you would have been so naughty. But Lord Devenham assures us that he is happy to be married to Emily. Was ever a man so forgiving! Such manners. Ah, that's the quality for you. I had thought we was socially ruined."

"Let us go into the drawing room a moment, Mama," said Mary, urging her back down the stairs.

"Now," said Mary, when they were both seated, "I am afraid the matter is serious. Emily is *not* married, for Mr. Cummings would be under the impression that *I* was the bride, and so . . ."

"No, no, *no,*" said Mrs. Anstey eagerly. "We thought that was the way of it. I did not pay much attention to what was going on, I was so excited, and neither did Mr. Anstey. First thing we knows is when it all came out in the vestry. But my lord, he ups and says he's happy with Emily. Upon which she fainted. . . ."

"Mama! This is monstrous. Emily must not . . ."

"Must not *what*?" demanded Mrs. Anstey crossly. "Mark my words, she fancies the earl for herself and is playing Miss Martyr to the hilt. How she talked you into it is beyond me."

"She drugged my morning chocolate."

"Ah," sighed Mrs. Anstey, with something like relief. "Then I have the right of it. I noticed the way Emily watched him, you know. She wanted him for herself."

"Let us go and see her," said Mary, folding her lips into a thin line. "She must be suffering quite dreadfully. She did not try to trick me. She did *suggest* the trick, but I refused to have any part of it, and so she put laudanum in my chocolate."

Cousin Bertha reluctantly surrendered her place at the top table to Mary.

Mary looked at Emily, and Emily smiled faintly and turned her head away. She had regained her normal rosy color and, although her manner seemed slightly stiff and formal, she did not look at all like a girl who had just found herself married to a man she did not like.

Puzzled, Mary looked next at Mr. Cummings. The blaze of love in his eyes warmed her heart despite her distress. Oh, if only it could turn out that Emily were *really* happy.

There was no opportunity to talk to Emily until much later. After the wedding breakfast, there was dancing, and everyone wanted to dance with the bride. The party became noisy as even the haughty relatives from the Devenham side of the family began to unbend under the effects of the Ansteys' lavish hospitality.

Mary found herself alone for a moment with Mr.

Cummings. In a hurried undertone, he told her of the scene in the vestry. Tears stood out in Mary's eyes.

"The marriage must be stopped, Mr. Cummings. It must be annulled."

"After the initial shock had worn off," said Mr. Cummings cautiously, "it appeared to me that Miss Emily was quite pleased to be a countess."

"Emily does not set any store in titles," said Mary. "Come with me. Let us try to get her away from the other guests for a little."

This proved to be more difficult than it should have been. Emily appeared to be avoiding her.

Strangely enough, the guests did not comment on the change of bride. The Devenham guests had referred to his bride-to-be as "that daughter of a counterjumper" ever since they had received the invitations and assumed that the common Ansteys had put the name wrongly on the wedding invitations "because that class of persons always does make mistakes like that."

The Anstey guests and relatives were puzzled, but did not dare say so, since it might turn out to be one of those upper-class ways of going about things which were so terrifying and so mystifying.

At last, Mary managed to pull Emily a little to one side. Mr. Cummings came up to join them.

"Emily," she said. "You cannot do this thing. Devenham must be quite mad, or his great pride makes him feel he must go along with it. The marriage *must* be annulled."

Emily seemed to sway a little toward her beloved sister. For one split second, Emily was about to throw herself on her sister's bosom and beg for help.

But in that split second, she saw Mr. Cummings take Mary's hand and give it a squeeze and saw all the love in their eyes as they looked briefly at each other, and her face became a careful mask.

"La! What a to-do you are making, Mary," laughed Emily. "*You* don't want him, and he is happy with me. You must not become jealous at this late date."

"Miss Emily," said Mr. Cummings, who felt that by not giving her correct title, he was showing her he had not accepted the marriage. "Do but listen. You are a very brave girl, but you must not make this sacrifice."

"You forget yourself, Mr. Cummings," said Emily in a flat voice. "In future, use my title when you address me. I am to be a countess—I *am* a countess— and I will make a much better one than Mary would have done." She flicked her sister's cheek with her long white fan. "If you ever want to raise your eyes higher than this village prelate, do but come and join me in London, Mary *dear*."

Emily drifted off, leaving them both scandalized.

"She is acting!" said Mary after she had furiously thought about her sister's outrageous behavior.

"Not she," said Mr. Cummings. "Just look."

Emily was hanging onto the earl's arm and flirting quite blatantly with him. The close-fitting wedding gown set off the trimness of her figure and the swell of her bosom.

The earl looked politely amused. It was hard to know what he was thinking.

"This may mean we can be married," said Mr. Cummings in a low voice.

Mary turned and looked at his plain, honest face, at the love in his eyes, and she felt dizzy and happy. Although she was still worried about Emily, although she could hardly believe Emily meant those words she had just said, Mary felt herself enveloped in a rosy cloud, alone with Mr. Cummings, while the guests walked and chattered and danced all about. Then, looming up like a black cloud on the horizon, came the earl of Devenham.

"I think you at least owe me one dance, Mary," he said.

Mr. Cummings looked confused. He wanted to protect Mary from embarrassment on the one hand, but, on the other, he could hardly begrudge the man a chance to ask for an explanation.

Mary allowed herself to be led onto the floor. It was a country dance, which mercifully allowed little chance for conversation. But when it was over and they were promenading before the next dance, the earl began in a mocking voice, "Well, love of my life, are you not even going to apologize for this charade?"

Poor Mary blushed to the roots of her hair. "I . . . did . . . I mean, I couldn't. Oh, I am so sorry."

"You do not love me."

"No more than you do me," said Mary sharply.

"Did you not think to tell me?"

"I felt I could not," said Mary. "I felt it would be so cruel and . . . and . . . all the guests had been invited. I would not have let this happen . . ."

"Emily told me she drugged you."

"You must not think badly of her. She was doing it to save me. Emily is very young."

"I do not know whether her distress after the wedding was because she was afraid of reprisals or whether she really was acting the part of the sacrificial lamb."

"The marriage must not stand," pleaded Mary. "Many other women would be proud to be your wife."

"But not you," he said dryly. "Have I changed so much?"

"Yes, you are like a stranger to me."

"Strange," he mused, "and yet the years have not touched you at all. You look the same, you *are* the same . . . except in one respect." His eyes flicked toward where Mr. Cummings stood anxiously at the edge of the floor.

Mary blushed. "I feel so foolish," she said. "It is not in my nature to be fickle. You must forgive me and forgive us all. Emily must not be made to suffer."

"Many ladies," said the earl with some asperity, "would not consider the prospect of being a rich countess as suffering."

"But Emily . . ."

"Have you spoken to your sister?"

"Yes."

"And she said . . . ?"

"Emily said she was content with the arrangement."

"I believe she is," he said. "It is an arranged marriage, a situation much more common than a love match. Perhaps 'twill serve."

"I do not know what to think," said Mary
wretchedly. "Mama and Papa are so happy that
their ambitions have not been ruined. I know their
ambitions may seem disgracefully worldly, but you
must agree, my lord, that they are not unusual in
that. It is the way of the world."

"Damn the world," said the earl of Devenham.
"I do not care for the rules of a world that is
bounded by Grosvenor Square and St. James's
Square. We will see what comes of it. I am not a
brute. I am at fault for insisting the wedding go
ahead. I shall, therefore, give Emily until eight this
evening, which is supposed to be the time when I
leave on my honeymoon, to come to a decision. If,
by that time, she does not wish to be my wife, I shall
take steps to have the marriage annulled."

"You are very generous," said Mary. "It is more
than we deserve."

"Perhaps I owe something to the memory of that
very green captain who was so very much in love."
He raised her hand to his lips.

Emily came up and put a possessive hand on the
earl's arm. "Flirting, Devenham?" she cried. "And
us newly wed? Fie, for shame, Mary."

"We owe Lord Devenham a great deal," said
Mary repressively. "Few men would be possessed
of such charity under the circumstances."

"Pooh!" laughed Emily. "I am neither hunch-
backed nor ill-favored. My lord has gained quite a
bargain. Come, Devenham. It is the waltz."

She went off on the earl's arm, throwing a laughing glance over her shoulder at Mary, who stood
rooted to the spot.

"I do not know this Emily *at all*," thought poor Mary, shaking her head in bewilderment.

When the time came for Emily to retire and change from her bride's clothes to her traveling dress, Mary followed her upstairs to her bedroom, hoping to find the old Emily waiting there. But Emily had a coterie of female guests about her and was laughing and chattering as if she did not have a care in the world.

She laughingly refused Mary's offer of the clothes that had been made for the trousseau. Mama was so generous, Emily said, that her own clothes were fit for any bride.

Attired in a figured sarsenet of white ground with small sprigs of pink color and wrapped in the very latest thing in cloaks—fine Bath coating, descending to the feet, with a large military cape and hood—and with a shade bonnet of fine brown cane with a high crown of brown satin, ornamented with chenille and velvet flowers perched on her head, Emily tripped lightly down the stairs to where her husband was waiting in his traveling carriage.

She stood with one foot on the carriage step, turned, threw her wedding bouquet into the crowd. Mary caught it, and held it to her bosom, her eyes wide and appealing as she looked at Emily, willing her not to go through with it if she did not want to.

For one moment, Emily caught her sister's intense gaze and the smile left her face. She made a half-movement as if to run back, and then, with a little shrug, waved her hand and climbed into the carriage.

The coachman cracked his whip, The guests cheered, and the well-sprung carriage moved off down the drive. Outside the gate, the villagers cheered and huzzahed. The carriage window opened and the earl threw out a handful of silver and copper.

The crowd cheered again.

Mary found Mr. Cummings at her elbow and leaned slightly against him for comfort, watching and watching until the carriage disappeared from sight.

Chapter Five

Silence reigned inside the carriage; thick black night, outside.

"Where are we bound?" asked Emily at last in a small voice.

"We are on our way to Maxton Court."

"To stay with friends?"

"Maxton Court, my love, is my new ancestral home."

"Oh."

"Yes, oh. Did Mary not even tell you where she was to spend her honeymoon?"

"No."

"Well, now you know."

"Is it far?"

"Two counties away. We will stop soon at a posting inn for the night."

Emily fell silent. The night ahead loomed up full of menace. What exactly were those mysterious marital rights? Would she be expected to kiss him a lot? It would not be all that bad, she thought, feeling very warm as she remembered that first kiss.

"My servant has ridden ahead to arrange accommodation for us," he said.

All at once, Emily thought longingly of her own bed at home—narrow, white, and virginal. How wonderful it would be if had been someone else's wedding, and, now that the guests were gone, she could sit with her feet on the fender and talk to Mary about the day's events.

A wave of homesickness assailed her as she leaned back and closed her eyes.

"Tired?"

"A little." Her eyes flew open at his question. This companion, this husband, would always be at her side. She stole a look at him. He was really very handsome when he was relaxed, as he was now. He could not have had the chance to have many affairs. He had returned several times on leave to London. He had not called on Mary during any of these visits home, since, prior to his earldom, there was no hope of the Ansteys inviting him.

He would, therefore, still have been a captain on those leaves, and Emily naively assumed London society to be as nice as the Ansteys in their choice of beaux for their daughters.

"Why, he is probably as innocent as I am myself!"

Much comforted by this thought, Emily began to relax.

Emboldened at last by the friendly silence of her

companion, she asked, "Were the Spanish ladies very pretty?"

"Some," came the answer.

"But Spanish society is very strict, more so than we are here, so it would not be possible for you to have had many . . . er . . . personal relationships."

"On the contrary. War breaks down many barriers of decorum." His eyes gleamed with mockery in the light from the carriage lamps.

"Oh," said Emily, pleating a fold in her gown. "But when you were on leave in London, it must have been so hard. I mean, the ton is so mercenary."

"And therefore I had to lead a celibate life? Not quite. I was a great favorite at balls and supper parties."

"You are teasing me," accused Emily.

"Not I. You cannot have everything, my sweeting. You have my title, my fortune, myself. You cannot expect virginity as well."

"Devenham!" shrieked Emily. "You should not speak thus. It is not fitting."

"I was catching the hook, my love. You were fishing."

"I was being polite . . . making conversation."

Emily slid a look at him out of the corner of her eyes. His face was closed, enigmatic. I have married a stranger, she thought. What on earth is going to happen tonight?

The inn was comfortable and well-appointed. Their private parlor was charming. Their bedroom had one large four-poster, which seemed to dominate the room.

Their servants had traveled in another carriage. The earl left to check that the horses were properly stabled for the night, and Emily seized his absence as the opportunity to change for dinner. Felice bustled about, warming a change of underclothes at the fire, heating the curling tongs on the portable stove, and looking as if she had not a care in the world.

Felice was happy because the second footman had promised her he would apply for a post in the Devenham household, and Felice herself was delighted to be appointed lady's maid to the new countess.

Emily would have loved to unburden some of her worries on the maid, but Felice was so neat, so efficient, and so *foreign* that Emily found she could not summon up the courage to say anything to the girl.

The earl entered the bedchamber soon after Emily was dressed and said that if she waited in the private parlor, he would join her.

Waiting beside the fire in the parlor, Emily drank two glasses of wine to fortify herself. When he eventually arrived, he had changed from his wedding clothes into a severe black coat with white cravat, black pantaloons, and striped stockings. As was the fashion, the pantaloons hugged his muscular legs, showing the ripple of each strong muscle under the cloth.

The earl was charming over supper. The earl was witty. The earl was very seductive. And the more charming, witty, and seductive he became, the more terrified Emily felt. His presence seemed to be assaulting all her senses at once. She felt overwhelmed by the increasing air of sensuality that seemed to emanate from his body.

Emboldened by the wine she had drunk, Emily did her best to laugh at his stories and parry his flirtatious remarks. But no amount of wine could drown the ever-present image of that large double bed.

At last, he came around the table and helped her from her chair.

"Go and prepare for bed," he said softly. "I will join you very shortly."

"Yes, Devenham," she whispered.

He put his arms around her and smiled as he felt her body tremble against his own. Mistaking her fear for the stirrings of passion, he said huskily, "Go to bed."

Emily trailed from the room. Once in the bedroom, she sat in a chair and stared at the bed. Felice entered quietly, and Emily waved her away. "I will undress myself, Felice," she said. "Do not come to me until the morning."

Felice curtsied and left.

"I *can't*," thought Emily. "This is dreadful." A whole unknown and threatening world of hot, masculine lust lay in waiting.

Like a sleepwalker, Emily got to her feet, wrapped her thick cloak around her, left the room, left the inn, and simply walked off, out into the night.

A thick, wet, November mist had fallen. She had only walked a few steps from the inn when she found herself wrapped in dripping blackness. Water dropped from the trees like tears and sparkled on her hair. The road was muddy and her thin silk slippers were soon ruined. She had no idea where she was going. She had one thought and one thought only—to put as great a distance between herself and the inn as was humanly possible.

Emily thought she heard footsteps behind her. The mist wavered and thinned a little, and by the faint yellow glow of candlelight from a cottage, which seemed to materialize at the side of the road, she saw a small road branching off. She turned onto it, quickening her pace.

The mist closed in again. At times, she could not even see the edge of the road, which was growing progressively rougher, and at one point she almost tumbled into the ditch at the roadside.

Water dripped and plopped mournfully from the trees, and chuckled in the ditch.

A dog leaped out of the bushes and ran snarling and snapping at her ankles. It caught the hem of her cloak, growling and worrying the cloth with its teeth.

She wrenched her cloak free and ran headlong down the road, until she was gasping for breath and had a painful stitch in her side.

When she finally slowed, she realized the road was gradually petering out into a grassy track.

She came to a five-barred gate with a thick thorn hedge on either side. Exhausted and unable to go any further, she sank down on a wet tussock of grass and huddled inside her cloak.

After a few moments, the icy cold began to seep into her very bones.

Emily got to her feet, wondering what to do. She did not want to retrace her steps for fear of meeting the dog or, worse—her husband. Stiffly and painfully, she put one sore foot on the first rung of the gate and began to climb.

When the earl of Devenham entered the bedroom and found it empty, his first thought was that his bride had gone out to the Jericho at the back of the inn, being too timid to use the chamberpot.

After a quarter of an hour had passed, he went in search of her, and, not finding her anywhere about the inn, came to the logical conclusion that she had run away.

His pride reeled under this fresh blow. She had looked so very pretty during supper with the candlelight gilding her hair that he had quite persuaded himself she had deliberately stolen a march on her sister by marrying him herself.

To reinforce that idea, there was her behavior at the wedding. And since he was not given to much self-hate, he could hardly be blamed for thinking that he must have *some* attraction. He was hardly the kind of man who would drive a young girl to sacrifice herself because the idea of her sister's marriage to him was so repugnant.

He only had had his title and fortune for a short time, but already he had noticed all the alchemy wrought by fortune and title.

In fact, ever since the Ansteys' harsh rejection of his suit those ten years ago, he had not really had to suffer any great humiliations. He was adored by his men. He was accounted a prime favorite with the ladies, and the Duke of Wellington had called him the best dancer in the army—high praise indeed, since the Iron Duke dearly loved his officers to be able to dance well. He had enjoyed the inter-

mittent favors of a mistress. Mrs. Cordelia Haddington had been pleased to welcome him into her
bedchamber and into her expert and clever hands
every time he returned to London on leave.

But the bed was empty. Emily was gone, her
nightdress and nightcap still laid out on the bed.

Having realized this humiliating fact, his first
desire was to go straight to bed and forget about the
whole thing. His second, to rouse the inn and the
countryside and get out men and dogs to join him
in the search.

His third was to try to find her himself.

He went downstairs, roused the landlord, and
asked if he could borrow a lantern, saying that
something of value had dropped from the carriage
and that he was going out on foot to look for it.

He refused the landlord's offer of servants to help
him in the search. The landlord, he knew, put his
lordship's refusal of help down to the eccentric
ways of the Quality. The earl felt he could bear
that.

What he was damned if he would stand for, until
it became inevitable, was the scandal and laughter
that would be caused when it became known that
his young bride had run off on her wedding night,
rather than suffer his lovemaking.

The earl's harsh countenance, albeit a handsome one, had, until that night, been misleading.
Although he had acquired an autocratic manner
and social veneer, there were still remnants of that
eager young captain he had once been. But Emily's
flight had effectively squashed the last grain of ro-
manticism and love in his character—or so he felt.
It was as if his outer casing were moving inward

until his whole body felt like a stone. The only fires that burned in him as he set out into the mist were the fires of anger.

Once clear of the inn, he diligently searched the mud of the roadway until he found what he was looking for, the marks of a pair of small, slippered feet.

He followed them carefully and patiently, forcing himself not to hurry in case he lost the track, cursing the clammy heaviness of the mist.

He almost lost the tracks at the turning in the road, but he finally picked up the trail again. A little way down a side road, the dog that had frightened Emily made a rush for his boots.

The earl stood stock-still. "Go away, you miserable cur," he said evenly, "or I'll kick you to death."

The dog bared its teeth in a yellow, ingratiating leer and slunk off into the bushes.

The earl held the lantern high, noticing that the footsteps in the mud were deeply indented at the toe. The dog must have frightened Emily and she must have started to run.

"Good," he thought nastily. "Serves her right, the ungrateful jade."

He carefully made his way along the road, following the erratic trail of footsteps which went at some points from one side of the road to the other.

He came to the five-barred gate. Again, he held the lantern high, and then, with an exclamation of impatience, shone the light over the gate, noticing that the footsteps went straight out across the ploughed field on the other side.

He swung himself lightly over the gate. He was

halfway across the field when he came upon one of Emily's slippers. He picked it up. It was a poor, tattered, muddy wreck and there was a faint trace of blood in the silk.

"She must be demented," he muttered, completely unable to understand why he had engendered such mad terror in anyone.

At the far end of the field, tussocky dry grass led into a pine wood. He searched this way and that for some clue as to which direction she had taken. He did not want to call out for fear she would go into hiding. His boots making no sound on the floor of pine needles in the wood, he continued to search, noticing that the mist had thinned and that faint silver moonlight was beginning to penetrate the wood.

He found her in a little glade.

He stood very still at the edge, thinking that she looked like a princess in a fairy tale.

She was lying in the grass with one arm thrown out. The moonlight illuminated the moving and shifting mist and her hair, cascading about her face, had turned to silver.

Then he noticed the way the rough grass sparkled like marcasite under the moon.

Frost.

He found himself wondering in a numb, detached kind of way whether she was dead.

The earl walked lightly across the glade and knelt down beside Emily. She was fast asleep with exhaustion. He was moved to a feeling of pity, but hard on the heels of his pity came the thought, If she has contracted the ague, then she might die and I will be free.

But that unworthy thought went as quickly as it had come.

He bent and picked her up in his arms. She opened her eyes and let out a low moan of terror.

"It is I," he said grimly. "Devenham."

Emily struggled weakly in his arms, but he paid no attention. He strode back the way he had come, the lantern dangling from one hand, as he cradled Emily's body in his arms. He did not need to use a lantern to light the way. The mist had lifted and, besides, he felt he knew every inch of the muddy track by heart.

Emily was asleep again. Again he felt pity for her, but fought it down. His sole aim was to get her into the inn without being observed.

Emily found herself being shaken roughly awake. They were outside the arch leading to the inn courtyard.

"Stand there," said the earl, "until I return for you. If you run away again, I will find you and *beat* you. Do I make myself plain?"

Emily nodded, her eyes wide with fear.

"Good!"

He strode off into the courtyard. Emily leaned her head against the rough stone wall. Her body felt strange and light, and the sounds from the inn seemed to reach her ears from over a very long distance.

The earl came back. In his hand he held a rough sack.

"Climb in," he ordered.

"Why?" said Emily, in sudden terror. "I know! You are going to throw me in the river."

"Much as I would like to," he said between his

67

teeth, "I am not. In order to avoid scandal, I told
the landlord that I had gone out to search for something that had dropped from the carriage. You are
that something. Get in this sack immediately and
do not utter one word until I get you upstairs."

He looked stern and forbidding, and, in any case,
Emily felt too weak to protest further.

She climbed into the sack. He tied the string at
the top and heaved her onto his back. Emily could
hardly breathe. The sack had contained grain of
some sort, and little particles of dry chaff went up
her nose with every breath she drew.

She was bumped against his back as he strode
across the inn courtyard.

"Evening, my lord," came the landlord's voice.
"Found what you were looking for?"

"Yes, thank you." The earl's voice. "I hope I did
not waken you."

"No, my lord. Expecting the mail coach any moment. No sleep for me this night. Allow me to carry
that."

"No, no. I am well able to handle it."

"Lucky it waren't stolen, my lord. I call to
mind . . ."

The earl dumped the sack on the floor. Emily
suddenly knew she was going to sneeze. The landlord's voice droned on and on, somewhere above her
head. Emily tried not to think about sneezing; she
tried pinching the bridge of her nose. It was no use.
The sneeze was coming. Ah . . . Ah . . . *Ah* . . . *oooof!*
The earl had kicked the sack, and his foot had
caught her on the side of the head. It had the effect
of stifling the sneeze at birth. The kick had been no
more than a nudge, but Emily began to think the

earl really meant to kill her. If you tied your wife up in a sack and then kicked her in the head, it followed that your feelings toward said wife were not of the sweetest.

At last, she felt herself being lifted up again.

"Looks uncommon like a dead pig you've got in there, m'lord," said the landlord.

"How very clever of you," came the earl's voice. "That is exactly what it is. I never go on any of my honeymoons without a dead pig."

"Eh? Ah, my lord. I was near taking you serious—like. That's a good 'un. I'll tell missus. I never goes on my honeymoon without a dead pig!"

His laughter followed them up the stairs. The earl opened the bedroom door and let out a sigh of relief. He opened the sack and released Emily by simply dragging the sack along the floor until it was clear of her.

"We will go into this matter in the morning, my lady *wife*," he said. "We are going to bed. Do not look so stricken. I have no intention of touching you."

Emily quailed before the blazing contempt in his eyes. She picked up her nightgown and cap and headed for the parlor door, meaning to change in the privacy of the other room.

He caught her by the hair and jerked her about. "Oh, no, you don't," he grated. "Stand still."

He took her cloak from her shoulders and threw it on a chair. He twisted her about and deftly untied the tapes at the back of her dress and the tapes at her waist. He removed her corset *élastique* and contemptuously pinged it across the room. She clutched desperately at her shift, but he said coldly,

"It either goes over you head or is ripped from your body. Take your pick, madam."

All at once, too tired, too numb with cold to feel ashamed, she raised her arms meekly above her head. He crumpled the shift into a ball, and then dropped her nightgown over her head.

"Sit down by the fire."

Emily sat down while he shoveled coals on the fire. He then carried over a water can and basin, slid off her torn stockings, and bathed her feet. It was all done deftly and impersonally.

He then picked her up, carried her to the bed, and tucked her in.

As he began taking off his own clothes, she turned and buried her suddenly hot face in the pillow. The terror of what he was about to do to her would, she was sure, effectively keep her awake, but her eyelids drooped and a welcome darkness engulfed her.

The earl climbed into bed and jerked the curtains closed. He lay with his hands behind his head, staring up at the canopy, which was gleaming red from the leaping flames of the fire.

Tomorrow, he would decide what to do with her. She moved in her sleep, murmured something, and then rolled over until she was lying pressed against the length of his body. She smelled faintly of soap and rose water and pine.

She did not wake up when he pushed her roughly away.

What do you do on the first day of your marriage when that marriage has not been consummated? Emily awoke in all the intimacy of the inn bedchamber. For one blissful moment, she thought she was at home. Then a faint sigh beside her brought her back to reality with a thud. Without even looking at her husband, she scrambled nervously from the bed, drawing the curtains tightly around the bed in case he should wake up and watch her dressing. She gave herself a perfunctory wash and scrambled into her clothes. Her first thought was to go out for a walk so as to escape the embarrassment of facing him when he woke up. But her second, saner thought was that he would probably be in a towering rage if he found her missing again. She dressed and, since he was still asleep, she began to wish she had made a more thorough toilet. Her stomach gave a faint protesting growl. Somewhere below, someone was grilling kidneys and frying bacon. It was agony sitting here waiting for him to wake up. Should she go into the parlor and order breakfast? Or ring for breakfast?

They talked incessantly at local assemblies about the enviable freedom of married women, thought Emily. Sitting here too frightened to move until the lord and master decided to wake up could hardly be called freedom. Emily looked longingly at the bellpull on the wall. One jerk of it and a little bell on the kitchen wall downstairs would ring; some blessed servant would arrive, and in that way he would wake up and she would not be alone with him.

Emily became very angry with herself for being so timid. A married lady would probably call her maid and go about things as usual. But not on the first morning of her honeymoon, said a treacherous voice in Emily's brain. So the obvious solution to the immediate problem was to wake him up. Perhaps he was already awake, lying behind those bed curtains, staring up at the canopy and working out plans of revenge.

Emily gave a timid little cough.

Silence.

She coughed again. Louder.

Silence.

The bed curtains did not move.

"Devenham!" she called softly.

Then loudly. "*Devenham!*"

Emily sank down in a chair by the window.

Perhaps he was dead. That would be very sad, of course, but she would be free. And she would still be the Countess of Devenham without any of the responsibilities. She would call the surgeon. She would be expected to cry. Well, that would not be so very difficult if only she remembered that kiss. And she would make sure he had a really splendid funeral. Perhaps he would have to be buried in Westminster Abbey. Black horses with black plumes to do justice his rank. And mutes. Mutes would have to be hired. But she would be expected to go to his home on her own and face all his servants. Perhaps they might blame her for his death. Perhaps she might be tried and sent to Tyburn! No, Tyburn scaffold was gone, and they now hanged people outside Newgate. But she was a peeress, so she might be executed at the Tower. The gates of the Tower clanged as she was led from the river up the damp steps.

There was the executioner's block and there was the executioner in his black mask. There was Mary, crying desperately. "She sacrificed herself for me," wailed Mary. The prince regent had come in person to witness this interesting execution. "Stay!" he cried. "I cannot bear to see one so fair die beneath the headman's axe."

"Your Highness," said Emily. "Although I did not kill him, I cannot bear to live without him. Please let the execution go forward."

Yes, that was terribly touching. Tears ran down Emily's face as she sat by the window.

"You brought it on yourself, you silly widgeon," said a sleepy voice at her ear.

"Devenham!" screamed Emily. She had been so immersed in her dream that it was horrifying to see the man she had so lately buried standing beside her clad only in a nightshirt.

"Who on earth did you expect to see?" said her husband crossly. "The way you go on, young lady, leads me to wonder whether you are touched in your upper works."

He walked over to the toilet table and began to pull his nightgown over his head.

"*Devenham!*"

"What *is* the matter? Are you going to sit there screaming Devenham all morning?"

"You are taking off your nightgown!"

"You have a great deal to learn about me that is interesting and strange," he said caustically. "I do not normally wear my nightgown under my clothes during the day. Strange, is it not?"

He wrenched off his nightgown. Emily took one horrified look at his well-muscled back and buried her hot face in her hands. There was a great deal of splashing, then the sound of him crossing the room, followed by the imperative summons of the

73

bell. After a few moments, the door opened and Emily lowered her hands as he heard the earl say, "You may barber me now."

While his Swiss got to work, Emily summoned up courage to ring for Felice. She began to relax as the French maid tut-tutted over the mess of her mistress's hair and began to set it to rights. At one point, Emily caught the maid and the valet exchanging a glance as if both were wondering about this strange wedding morn. After her hair had been carefully curled and styled and her face and arms bathed in warm water and cologne, Emily felt that the day might not be quite as bad as she expected.

My lord and my lady were informed that breakfast awaited them in their private parlor. Emily did not know whether to be glad or sorry that there was not much opportunity for conversation, since the earl had his nose buried in the morning paper.

At last he lowered the newspaper. "What shall we do today, Devenham?" asked Emily brightly.

He drained his tankard of small beer and looked at her thoughtfully. She was looking very beautiful, if a little pale. Her gown of blue silk velvet enhanced her blond beauty and the purity of her skin. The earl sighed. When he had planned this honeymoon he had meant to spend most of the first day in bed and then, on the following day, travel to his country home. He shrugged. "I do not know, my lady. This is market day in Market Warborough, which is the nearest town. Perhaps I might go to see if there is something interesting in the way of horseflesh. You may come if you wish."

The day matched Emily's mood, being cold and

gray, with the bare branches of the trees rattling in an icy wind. They made their silent way to Market Warborough, finally stopping at an inn in the very center of the town. Everything was noise and bustle, farmers and their wives, horse dealers, shepherds and market women, all jostling along the narrow, cobbled lanes under the shadow of the overhanging Tudor buildings. What long and mysterious conversations the gentlemen seemed to have about horses.

Emily stood patiently with her toes beginning to ache with cold and her nose turning first pink and then blue. Finally the earl became aware of her patient waiting.

"Go back to the inn," he said, "and I will join you shortly."

Emily made her way back to the inn and then stood inside the door, wondering what to do. Everyone seemed to be very merry, very loud, and very drunk, and there was not another lady in sight.

A buck looked out of the open taproom door and called, "Venus in our midst, fellows. A veritable Venus!"

Emily was soon surrounded by beery, grinning faces. Her clothes were of a fine enough quality to stop her admirers from more open insult, but on the other hand, she had no maid and no husband, so the throng pressed closer and the jokes became warmer.

"You are all disgusting and drunk," said Emily, goaded beyond endurance. "You cannot hold your drink like a gentleman should . . . or even a lady for that matter. I swear I could drink any of you under the table!"

To her horror, this was taken as a challenge; she was swept into the tap and a glass of wine thrust into her hand. She looked wildly about and prayed that Devenham would come to rescue her. How *could* he desert her so?

The Earl of Devenham had just finished buying a splendid-looking bay and was giving instructions to deliver it to his home when a stout farmer's wife tapped him on the shoulder with her umbrella. "Sir," she said. "Do you have anything to do with the pretty young miss with the yaller hair? Is it Your Honor's daughter perhaps?"

"My wife," said the earl curtly. "What about her?"

"Them ruffians has got her in the tap and the poor little lady's drinking something cruel. My Bill said he couldn't stand no more of it, and he sent me direct to . . ."

But she spoke to the open air, for the earl was already off and running.

Emily was in a state of euphoria. What jolly, splendid gentlemen they all were! And how missish she had been to be afraid of them. She drained another glass of burgundy in one long swallow and smiled mistily at the subsequent roar of applause.

Then she blinked. Where had all the cheery gentlemen gone? One moment she had been surrounded by her cheering admirers, and the next, they had faded away. She swayed and clung to the back of the chair.

"You are in no fit state to answer my questions at the moment, madam," grated the earl. "Come!"

Emily let go of the back of the chair, took one step forward, and fell in a heap on the floor.

He picked her up in his arms, and she smiled dizzily up at him laying her head against his shoulder.

"We will go to my home, Maxton Court, on the morrow," he said, "but tonight you will learn to behave like a wife."

The journey back came to Emily in flashes of consciousness before she dropped off into a drunken sleep.

Then she felt him carrying her upstairs.

She tried to struggle awake as she felt his fingers busy with the tapes of her gown. Cold air fanning down her body made her realize she was naked. She tried to scream in alarm, but only a mumble of protest came out.

The Earl of Devenham stripped off his own clothes and then lay down beside his wife.

He gathered her in his arms.

"Now, madam," he said.

Snore . . .

Emily was fast asleep.

He pushed her away and, climbing out of bed again, lifted her and covered her with the bedclothes. He got back in beside her and stared at the ceiling as Emily snored gently beside him.

"I have married not only the wrong sister," he said, "but a drunkard as well!"

Chapter Six

Maxton Court loomed up dark and forbidding against a steel gray sky.

"My grave," thought Emily with a shudder. "He is going to kill me."

But the future murderer said in a normal voice, "This is our home. It once belonged to a family called Maxton, but they all died out."

"It is very *black*," ventured Emily uneasily. He did not reply. A rising wind rattled the trees lining the drive.

Maxton Court had been built in the reign of James I. It had a moat and drawbridge, since the first Maxton had not quite believed that guns and cannon were here to stay, despite the fact that both had been around for some time before he had had the house built, and he believed strongly in moats, boiling oil, and armor for protection.

The whole rambling building was smothered in ivy, which fluttered and moved restlessly in the wind, giving the building the odd effect of being in motion. The moat had been drained. When Emily looked down as the carriage rattled over the bridge, she could see a herd of deer grazing beside bales of hay on the cropped grass.

The servants were all lined up in the vast draughty entrance hall to meet their new mistress. The earl was pleased to note that Emily behaved very prettily. The servants were amazed at the new Lady Devenham's youthful appearance, since they had all heard of the earl's youthful romance. Exactly how they had heard of his early love was hard to tell, since the earl had never spoken of it, but servants' gossip had a truly marvelous way of carrying a very long distance.

Emily was relieved to find she had a private bedchamber and drawing room. Felice chattered happily as she set about unpacking her mistress's belongings. La! It was dark and cold. And *old*.

Emily answered automatically. What did this husband of hers plan to do with her?

She had awakened feeling both ill and hungry. Try as she would, she could not remember anything after the first few glasses of wine in the taproom at Market Warborough. She had imagined all sorts of horrors. But Felice had somewhat reassured her by saying that my lord had carried Emily upstairs, as far as she knew, without waking her.

The earl had hardly spoken on the journey to Maxton Court.

A footman scratched at the door to announce supper, and Emily hastily finished her toilet and followed him downstairs and then along cold, shadowy passages.

The dining room was immense and faced north. A huge fire, big enough to roast an ox, did little to alleviate the pervading chill.

The earl was in evening dress and already seated at one end of the long table. Emily sat at the other and stared at her husband across a long, narrow stretch of white linen, silver, and glass.

They ate their way through dish after dish, Emily barely tasting her food.

The tablecloth was then removed and the fruit, nuts, and wine brought in. The servants retired.

The earl spoke. "If you will pour yourself a glass of wine, you may send it down to me."

Emily looked nervously at the little silver wagon on wheels at her elbow, which contained three decanters: port, sherry, and madeira. She poured herself a glass of madeira, carefully put the crystal decanter back on the wagon, and gave it a push. One of the wheels appeared to have jammed. The earl sighed and rapped one long finger on the table.

She gave it an enormous push. The old floors of the house were uneven and the dining room was on a definite slope. The wagon set off decorously enough, but it gathered momentum as it sped down the long, polished table. The earl put out his hand a second too late. It flew past him and sailed off the end of the table, continued on its journey, and crashed into the far wall.

"I am *so* sorry," babbled Emily, "but you see . . ."

"No matter," said the earl. He stood up and went to retrieve the wagon. The contents were miraculously undamaged. He carried it back to the table and poured himself a glass of port.

Emily began to giggle nervously. The earl raised his thin eyebrows. Emily began to laugh, and the more supercilious her husband's expression became, the harder she laughed. "We look so *silly*," she gasped at last.

"I beg your pardon," he said.

"There you are!" shouted Emily. "You can barely hear me, which is not in the slightest amazing, since you are seated about a mile away."

The earl picked up the decanter in one hand and his glass in the other and walked down the length of the table, pulled out a chair next to Emily, and sat down.

Emily's laughter died abruptly, and she shrank back in her chair.

"Now," he said evenly, "we have a great deal to discuss."

"Yes, Devenham," whispered Emily.

She hung her head, her blond curls tumbling about her face. Her evening gown of gold silk was cut low enough to show the rapid rise and fall of two excellent breasts. He wrenched his eyes away and stared stonily down the table. The tremendous attraction she held for him was, he was sure, the result of overlong celibacy. Any woman who was not precisely an antidote would have held the same attraction.

"The situation is this," he said, taking a sip of wine and placing the glass carefully on the table. "We are locked in a marriage that is distasteful to both of us. This was brought about by your childish play-acting and interference."

Emily flushed with anger. She felt her action had not been without a certain amount of nobility.

"But, here we are. I expect you to learn the role of a countess. That is not too much to ask. I expect you to entertain with dignity and decorum such guests as I may choose. You will not see much of me. I have a great deal to do.

"*If* you behave yourself in what I may judge a suitable manner, then you may be allowed to go home on a short visit. I do not want your family here. If I decide that you have fulfilled your side of the bargain, then I might take you to London for the coming Season. I will eventually want an heir. But we will leave that side of things until later."

"And what is your side of the bargain?" demanded Emily.

"What?"

"You heard me. You have discussed *my* side of the bargain. What do you see as yours?"

The earl frowned. He thought hard. He could not really see that there *was* another side of the bargain. He felt he had behaved in an amazingly charitable and dignified manner. But she was looking at him, her wide brown eyes fixed on his face.

He cleared his throat. "For my part," he said, "I will behave to you in public as any faithful and devoted husband would. You will be allowed a certain amount of pin money for clothes and trinkets and those rubbishy books you like to addle your brains with."

"I am going to be very lonely," said Emily, thinking of the endless rooms and corridors in this black mansion. "I would like a pet. A dog or a cat."

"No," he said firmly. "Dogs belong in the kennels and cats in the stables or kitchens to keep down the rats. I cannot tolerate animals who do not work."

"It's a great wonder you manage to live with yourself," muttered Emily.

"I work very hard, that is when I am not engaged in marrying the wrong person. It is time for you to leave me to my port."

"Gladly."

He arose and assisted Emily from her chair. "There is one more thing, Devenham," she said, putting a timid hand on his sleeve. He looked at the hand with such rigid distaste that she quickly withdrew it.

"Yes?" he demanded, wondering what piece of trivia she was going to request. Her next words brought home to him with force that he was never going to know what to expect next from this wife of his.

"Are you going to kill me?" she said.

"Am I . . .? Don't be so gothic. How could you think of such a thing!"

"Easily," said Emily, calm now that she had got the dreadful words out. "You tied me up in a sack and you *kicked me in the head.*"

"I tied you up to save scandal. I was not aware which part of your anatomy I was kicking. I heard the preliminaries of a sneeze and was doing my best to put a stop to it. Had I known where I was kicking, then I should have kicked you in the nose."

"Brute!"

"Modify your language, ma'am. Besides, I did not kick you; I nudged you with my foot."

"You kicked me," said Emily, looking mulish.

"I did not! I . . ." He closed his mouth in a thin line. He had never understood, until now, why married couples went in for endless, pointless arguments about who did what to whom. Now he felt he knew.

He sat down at the table again and picked up his glass.

Emily curtsied to the back of his head and stalked out of the room.

Upstairs, Emily composed herself and sat down to write a lying letter to Mary. For a time Emily was happy as she penned the fiction of how content she was, gradually building up a picture of an ideal marriage.

When she had finished, she firmly sanded and sealed the letter, and then turned her thoughts to the predicament she was in.

Well, it was not so bad after all, she told herself. She was a countess, and that must count for *something*. Then she had this lovely home. At that moment, the wind whistled in the ivy and blew a puff of smoke down the chimney. Emily picked up a shawl and wrapped it around her shoulders. Lovely home, she repeated firmly.

The furniture in the bedroom was dark, massive, and Jacobean. I don't believe a new stick has been added to this place since the house was built, thought Emily. It would be fun to redecorate. But probably old fusty-dusty Peregrine likes it just the way it is. Nonetheless, it was an ancestral home. Next, she was not immediately threatened with any of those terrifying intimacies of marriage. And thirdly, she might find some jolly friends among the local county to lighten the tedium of her days. For the first time in her life, she would be socially acceptable.

Telling herself that things were really not too bad at all, Emily went to bed. But it was a long time before she slept. Despite Devenham's promise, she could not help waiting and watching the door, expecting him to enter at any moment.

She lay rigid, as, at last , she heard him mounting the stairs. But he passed her rooms and went to his own, his even step in the passageway outside not slackening its pace for a moment.

Then Emily slept.

During the next few weeks, Emily was kept very busy. She had not yet learned the gentle art of saying she was not at home to callers, and so the drawing room at Maxton Court often had as many as ten people at a time.

As news got about of the pretty little countess's hospitality, more people began to call, people who had never set foot in Maxton Court before, but Emily was not to know that.

She carefully kept a log of all her callers, together with their cards, so that she would have something to talk to her husband about in the evenings.

But the earl was absent. He spent most of the day about the estates. He went to a boxing match in the next county. He went to London for two weeks. On his fleeting appearances at home, he had his supper on a tray in the library.

The weather was cold and still, the whole countryside frozen under a thick coating of frost, which burned and glittered under a red winter sun.

Bored and restless, Emily ordered out the carriage and began to make calls herself.

There was the vicar, Mr. Graham, and his wife Martha, and their brood of children in the shabby vicarage. A dull but pleasant visit.

Then there were the Misses Parsons, two spinster ladies who lived in genteel poverty in a damp cottage under the shadow of the church. A most enjoyable visit.

The squire, Sir Basil Leech, and his two fat and jolly daughters came next on the list. After them, Lord and Lady Nightingale, chilly and grand and condescending. They had heard of the new countess's lowly origins. Emily decided not to call again.

Mindful of her new duties, she turned her attention to the tenant farmers and farm laborers. It was about this time that Emily began to enjoy herself. She was a good listener and had been starved for company. She like helping people and was amazed at how grateful they could be for the smallest attention. She started to set out with saddlebags full of medicine from the still room, cakes, biscuits, and sweetmeats from the kitchen, and wine from the cellars.

She gave only to the needy, not wanting to be accused of giving away her husband's provender to people who did not need it.

Her fussy, dainty clothes began to irk her, and so she mostly wore riding dress of a mannish cut, with a little hard hat with a veil on her head.

She sometimes thought uneasily that her husband would not approve of all this socializing with the farm laborers, and cringed when he appeared back from town one day, obviously having come in search of her, to find her on the floor of a laborer's cottage, playing with the baby.

But he only said mildly that he had come to escort her home.

Nonetheless, he looked so grim and forbidding that Emily's heart plumped right down to her serviceable boots. She would not admit to herself that the memory of that one and only kiss often came to plague her during the long cold nights, and that, at times, the sexlessness of her marriage made her feel less than a woman.

She decided the earl was angry because he obviously thought her enjoyment in the laborer's cottage was simply because she herself came from a lowly background.

The earl had, in fact, received a severe jolt in the solar plexus at the sight of his wife. The very mannishness of her dress made her seem extremely sweet and feminine. Stopping off at the inn before journeying home, he had heard of her great popularity in the village.

He was amazed and delighted at Emily's behavior, and, yes, he had to admit, he was proud of her. The charms of Mrs. Cordelia Haddington, which he had savored not so long ago, had done much to drive the humiliations of the Ansteys from his mind. Since Mrs. Haddington was a society widow and definitely not a member of the Fashionable Impure—or he would not have been able to afford her in the days of his captaincy—he knew that she had hoped for marriage and had rather dreaded a scene.

But the generous Cordelia had welcomed him back into her life, her bed, and her clever, clever hands without so much as a murmur of complaint. He enjoyed her witty, malicious tongue and her understanding sympathy, and before he knew what he was about, he had told her of the trials and complexities of his marriage.

Now, with Emily beside him in his carriage, he felt he had been disloyal, and paradoxically blamed Emily for that uncomfortable feeling.

Emily became increasingly gloomy because she *smelled* another woman. It was not that her husband reeked of scent. It was a certain relaxed air about his body and a *used* look about the skin of his lips, and, oh, nothing she could really explain.

But his next words surprised her. "I am very pleased with your behavior, Emily. Your calls on our tenants are much appreciated, and it will save me a great deal of work if you will write me a list of those in need of care and if anyone has been complaining about the lack of repairs to his property. I can then attend to things myself when you are gone."

"Gone? Gone, where?"

"Home. I thought you would enjoy a visit to your sister."

The earl looked surprised when a shadow crossed Emily's face. He did not know Emily was dreading returning home, where she would have to act the part of that silly Emily she had played at the wedding.

"And what will *you* do?" she asked.

"Do? I have plenty to do. The land must be clayed and marled, and I want to introduce the method of four-crop rotation. This way, I will be able to grow wheat where only rye has grown before. We must have improved animals and modern farm implements. Starving workers make bad workers, as starving soldiers make bad soldiers. The welfare of our tenant farmers and their laborers must be studied. Education for the children must be organized. Stupid farmers are also bad farmers."

"And what about *her*?" asked Emily in a thin little voice. "Will *she* be arriving as soon as my trunks are packed?"

He flashed her a look and continued as if he had not heard. "Salmon, the Duke of Bedford's surveyor, has invented many farm machines that I would like to see used here. . . ."

"You did not answer my question."

"I never answer questions in bad taste."

He stretched his long legs in their riding boots.

Emily burned with jealousy, although she did not yet recognize the emotion that was making her so angry.

This was *her* property, this husband. He was so formidable and austere it seemed unbearable to think that any other woman had had the magic to make those firm lips cover her own, to make that long hard body . . .

Tears flowed into Emily's eyes and she turned her head away.

"Yes, I will go home," she said.

The Elms was unchanged in that all the furniture and wallpaper had been changed. Emily's old, narrow bed had been thrown out and a large four-poster put in its place, no doubt to accommodate the extra body when she brought her husband home.

Emily allowed herself to be paraded before the local county, to the delight of her parents. She delighted them further by adopting the worst of her husband's manner. Mary privately thought Emily was behaving very badly indeed, but Mr. and Mrs. Anstey assured each other gleefully that their little Emily was every inch a countess now and had learned to sneer in a way that put everyone else in the shade.

Mary looked forward to getting Emily to herself so that she could find out what was really going on, but, to her horror, Emily carried her new countess manner into the house and up the stairs. It was like having some awful stranger in the house.

The fact that Christmas was to fall during Emily's visit home seemed to be the only thing that Mary could see that cracked the icy facade her sister wore. Mary was sure Emily felt she, Emily, should be at Maxton Court for Christmas.

The earl had been generous with his pin money, so Emily was able to buy expensive presents, although that was not such a novelty since she had always been very well provided for. Emily was plagued by visions of Christmas celebrations at Maxton Court, with that unknown lady taking her place at table and welcoming the local county.

The marriage had not been consummated. That much Emily knew, although she still did not know what consummation entailed. Devenham could call his lawyers and have the marriage annulled.

Then you would be free, her ever-active conscience pointed out.

Not without a fight, replied her illogical emotions.

You're like a dog with a bone, snapped her conscience. *You don't want him but you don't want anyone else to have him.*

What's wrong with that? sneered her emotions.

And so the battle went on in Emily's head as Christmas with its attendant celebrations came and went. Devenham had said he would send the carriage for her, but December moved into January and the carriage did not come. Emily grew weary of acting the part of a haughty countess. She grew thinner and paler.

"There is something badly wrong with her," Mary confided to Mr. Cummings. "It is like living with an *actress.*"

"Our marriage will not have any shadow over it," said Mr. Cummings, and kissed her so passionately that Mary forgot about her sister's troubles, for a time at least.

When Mary returned home and was passing Emily's room, she heard to her dismay the sound of noisy weeping.

She quietly pushed open the door and went in. The room was in darkness. She lit the candles and turned to the sobbing figure on the bed.

"Emily, it is I, Mary. What is the matter?"

"He remembered my Christmas present," came a harsh, muffled voice from the bed.

"Devenham? The roads have been bad, Emily. It is possible . . ."

"Look!" Emily raised a tear-stained face from the pillow.

A jewel box lay open on the bed. A gold and garnet necklace winked in the candlelight.

"It is exceedingly pretty," said Mary.

"Read the letter."

Mary picked up a crumpled piece of parchment and smoothed it out.

"Dear Emily," she read. "A favor for your Christmas. The carriage will come to take you home on the twenty-second of this month. D."

"I do not see what distresses you so," said Mary cautiously. "He wrote to me thus, if you will remember. It does not seem to be in his nature to write words of love."

"You are right," said Emily, mopping her eyes. "It was just that I thought perhaps the long absence would . . ."

"Make the heart grow fonder," Mary finished the sentence for her. "Emily, tell me the truth. I have consoled myself with the thought that you were happy, although you seemed to have grown exceedingly haughty and hard. I am to marry Mr. Cummings, and all because of your brave action. We have not yet asked Papa, but I am sure he will give us permission. Please tell me the truth about your marriage."

"Oh," said Emily wretchedly, "I did not want you to know. There is nothing very wrong. It is only . . ."

She told Mary the whole story. How she had run away on her wedding night, how angry Devenham had been, and how she suspected he had another woman in keeping.

"You must not go back," said Mary firmly. "I will tell Papa that his lawyers must have the mar-

riage annulled. Since you have not had a wifely re-
lationship with him, the matter should be easily
resolved. Calm yourself, Emily, there is no need to
return."

Emily's lips were set in a mutinous line. Mary
did not understand. If her husband had not missed
her, then a lot of other people would—the tenants,
the Misses Parsons, oh, so many. And she was his
wife. No other woman was going to take that role
away from her without a fight.

"I am going back," she said.

"I will not let you!" cried Mary. "You have suffered enough."

"I am not suffering," said Emily wearily. "My
nerves are overset. I do not think I could live here
again, Mary. I love you, and, yes, I do love Mama
and Papa. But around Maxton Court, there are so
many people, so many useful things to do. I could
not possibly return to this monotonous existence."

But Mary, who now thought Malden Grand the
most beautiful place in the world, since it contained Mr. Cummings, would not be persuaded. It
was all very simple. Devenham had turned out to
be an ogre, Emily was wretched, and therefore
some means must be found to terminate the marriage. Mary resolved to speak to their parents
about it in the morning.

She tried to argue with Emily, but got no further.

Left alone at last, Emily berated herself for her
weakness. She had only to wait until the twenty-
second. "But that's tomorrow!" screamed an
alarmed voice in her head. Her first thought was
to call Mary back. But then she realized all that

Mary would do would be to redouble her entreaties for her young sister to stay.

Emily rang the bell for Felice and told her to start packing immediately, deliberately ignoring the sullen look on the French maid's face. Felice's second footman was still in the Anstey household and had so far shown no signs of seeking employment at Maxton Court.

In the next room, Mary, exhausted with worry, had fallen asleep, and so was not aware of the frantic bustle of packing going on in Emily's bedroom.

Emily carefully wrapped her own Christmas present for her husband, thinking guiltily that she had not even sent it yet, although she had been upset that he had been late in sending hers. It was a diamond stickpin, a diamond of the first water, bought in the city by her complacent father, who had had it set at the local jeweler's.

The Anstey household was startled next morning by the arrival of the Earl of Devenham's coach, which rolled up the drive shortly before breakfast. In all the flurry of good-byes and partings, Mary did not have time to protest.

Mary quailed at the idea of telling her parents the truth of Emily's marriage. They were so proud and happy, and Emily had re-donned her haughty countess mask.

But as the carriage rolled away, Mary took a last look at the thinner, paler Emily who sat wrapped in furs, languidly waving her hand, and resolved that no time should be lost. After sending a servant to fetch Mr. Cummings, she went indoors to call a council of war.

Chapter Seven

The day was still and cold, with a lowering sky threatening snow. The Earl of Devenham's well-sprung carriage rumbled over the frost-hard roads, setting a good pace.

Opposite Emily, Felice was fast asleep, her head rolling with the motion of the carriage. The maid had regained her spirits. The second footman had promised to join her as soon as possible, and it was a very fine thing after all to be lady's maid in a noble mansion.

They were to break their journey at the same inn in which Emily had spent her wedding night

The horses suddenly swerved, and the nearside wheels went into a ditch. Adjusting her hat, Emily soothed Felice, who had wakened with a scream of alarm, crying, "Highwaymen!"

"It is probably a rock or a patch of ice on the road," said Emily soothingly.

The carriage dipped and swayed as the coachman and servants climbed down from the roof. The coachman's beefy face appeared at the window.

"Twere a cat, my lady. Just a scrap of a thing. If my lady would alight, we'll put turf under the wheels and pull the carriage clear."

"Where is the cat? Is it hurt?" asked Emily, climbing down stiffly onto the hard road.

"Not it, my lady. Pesky thing's over there in the ditch."

While Felice stood outside the carriage, anxiously looking up and down the road for highwaymen, Emily made her way over to the ditch on the other side of the road. Behind her, the servants were getting to work, sliding turf and stones under the wheels to give them purchase.

Miaow. A weak, plaintive sound. Emily parted some stalks of long, frozen grass and looked down. A little kitten looked up at her with a green, unwinking stare. It was painfully thin, and one ear was torn. Its gray coat was striped with black, and when it moved slightly, its small bones stood out sharply against its dusty fur.

"Oh, you poor thing," said Emily, kneeling down on the road, unmindful of the damage to her gown. She held out her hand. The kitten sniffed it cautiously.

Emily reached into the grass and picked the kitten up and held it to her breast, protecting it from the cold with her large fur muff. It half closed its eyes and began to purr, a roaring sound which seemed to vibrate through the whole of its small, starved body.

"You are coming with me," muttered Emily.

"And I don't care what *he* says. In any case, you'll be better off in the kitchens at Maxton Court than out here in the cold." The kitten purred louder, and with its purring, a little of the anguish and loneliness left Emily's young heart.

Felice came up, her black eyes snapping. "Put that nasty thing down, my lady," she exclaimed. "*Tiens!* Think of the fleas!"

With a lurch, the carriage behind them regained the road and two footmen rushed to open the door to help the ladies inside.

"I'm taking this cat with me," said Emily, climbing into the carriage.

"But my lady, 'tis well known his lordship does not like animals in the house. This I know, for the housekeeper, Mrs. Macleod, she tell the butler, and he . . ."

"Felice! I am taking this animal with me. I have said so. That is enough!"

Felice eyed the kitten nervously. Felice did not like animals and hated cats. Before she had come to work for the Ansteys, she had been lady's maid to a Mrs. Baxter who had had five of the beasts, and it had been Felice's job to groom the horrible cats as well as her mistress, which was the reason Felice had left to join the Anstey household.

The Anstey home had pleased Felice's housewifely, French soul. Everything was so new, so clean, so free from fur and hair.

The maid decided to keep silent. But when they stopped for the night, she would find some way to chase the animal away. One animal, Felice thought dismally, would lead to another and another, and then her whole day would be spent chopping liver and carrying saucers of milk.

As if to underline this thought, her young mistress said thoughtfully, "We will soon be stopping for the day, so we will be able to nourish this poor, starved thing."

To Felice, the poor starved thing's answering purr was like the roar of a lion.

"I will call you Peter," said Emily to the cat, "because you are like a little rock, a little rock by the roadside."

Felice closed her eyes in despair. Once they started talking nonsense like that, it was the beginning of the end. These English! Put the cat on a cushion and put the children to work in the manufactories.

Then she found something to distract her from worrying about the cat. "Look, my lady," she exclaimed. "Look at the snow!"

"Good heavens!" said Emily. "I hope we reach safety. One can hardly see."

Great, white, roaring sheets of snow were rapidly blotting out the landscape. She stood up and opened the trap in the roof, gasping as the icy snow-laden air struck her face. "John!" she called. "How far to The Green Man?"

"Only about five miles, my lady," came the coachman's reassuring shout. "Master reckoned the weather might be bad, and so he said to rack up not too far from Malden Grand."

"There you are," said Emily to Felice. "We shall soon be safe. Whether we can continue our journey on the morrow is another matter."

Not that he will care if I get lost in a snowdrift,

said a dismal little voice inside her head, and she hugged the kitten for comfort.

Cap in hand, Farmer Althorp stood in the earl's estate office earlier that day. His head was singing with all the talk of new crops and improvements. "Well, my lord," he said, touching his forelock, "It's all very interesting. The old earl, he never really troubled his head about such matters," said the farmer, implying that this was just the way a real earl was supposed to behave.

Farmer Althorp hesitated in the doorway. "We will be seeing her ladyship soon?" he asked, and then blushed, mentally cursing his wife for nagging him into being impertinent.

But the earl replied, mildly enough, "I am expecting Lady Devenham tomorrow. She sets out from her home today."

"Never today!" said the farmer.

"Why not?"

"There's a great snowstorm coming, my lord."

"Are you sure?" The earl's features became sharp with anxiety. Farmer Althorp's ability to forecast the weather was already a legend in the county.

"Mortal sure, my lord."

After the farmer had left, the earl sat looking out of the window at the lowering sky. If Farmer Althorp said there was going to be a bad storm, then he meant it was going to be very bad indeed. The earl ran over in his mind the servants he had sent to collect Emily. The coachman, John, was old but had a good head on his shoulders. The groom was a strong young man, and the two footmen were surely young and healthy enough to see to the safety of their mistress. But they had all been trained to obey his every command, and his command had been that they should rack up at The Green Man. Fortunately, The Green Man was only a short journey from Malden Grand, and he had warned them to make the journey in easy stages if the weather looked bad. So there was no cause for concern.

But it was not possible to imagine Emily behaving herself.

She was very young and quite hen-witted. Then he had to admit that he had tried his best not to miss her, only to find, to his fury, that he thought about her quite a lot.

He had spent Christmas not at Maxton Court but in London with his mistress, Mrs. Cordelia Haddington. Since it was quite *comme il faut* to have a mistress, no matter how newly married one was, and because Mrs. Haddington was a lady of the ton, he had been seen in her company at many society events. It was not as if tonish gossip would reach the unfashionable Ansteys of Malden Grand, he had thought, quite forgetting that the Ansteys had become fashionable by dint of his marriage to one of their daughters.

Mrs. Haddington's charms had seemed too full-blown, and her manner had become increasingly possessive. The more guilty the earl felt about betraying Emily, the more determined he became to prove to himself that she did not mean anything to him. Let her perish in a snowdrift.

But he was really not very surprised to find himself in the stables ten minutes later, ordering his horse to be saddled and telling his Swiss, John Phillips, to get ready to accompany his master.

They were halfway on their road and not one snowflake had fallen. The earl began to feel like a fool, and was on the verge of turning back.

Then one little flake brushed against his cheek, then another, and another.

"Here it comes, m'lord," shouted the Swiss. And here it did come—a great, white, blinding blizzard.

The earl bent his head before the storm and urged his horse to go faster.

The early winter's evening was closing down when Emily, Felice, and the servants struggled on foot to the inn. It seemed amazing that they had lost their way and managed to end up in the middle of a field, but that was where the earl's carriage was resting, half-buried in the snow. Despite Emily's protests, the servants had insisted on bringing the trunks. They had elected to walk rather than risk being thrown from a stumbling horse into a drift. The coachman brought up the rear, leading the horses. Emily led the way with the cat, Peter, hidden in her muff. In her other hand, she was carrying a bandbox by its ribbons.

It was the early darkness that had guided their footsteps, because, through the whirling nightmare of snow, they had caught glimpses of the lights of the village.

The landlord came bustling out to meet them, assuring them of roaring fires and good food. "And some milk and food for my cat," said Emily.

"Well, now, my lady, if you'll just give me the creature, I'll take it along to the kitchens."

"No," said Emily firmly. "I want it here with me."

Felice rolled her black eyes to the rafters. Cat mania was setting in early.

Emily felt they were all too exhausted to stand on ceremony and insisted that after the horses were rubbed down, fed, and stabled, they should all eat together in the dining room of the inn.

She regretted her democratic impulse after the food had been served. Felice was quite at ease, although her black eyes kept sliding to the cat, crouched on the floor and noisily lapping at a saucer of milk. But the menservants were silent and awkward, and Emily realized that they would have been much happier without her. But she was too hungry to really care.

At last Felice excused herself, saying she wished to go abovestairs to see to the unpacking of my lady's trunks.

"And I will take your little cat with me," Felice crooned, bending over Peter, who crouched away from her.

"Leave him," said Emily. "I will bring him up in a minute."

"But it is better to do it quietly, no?" urged Felice. "These landlords, often they not like animals in the bedchambers."

"Very well," said Emily. "I will join you shortly. Oh, do not be so *rough*, Felice!" For Felice had seized the cat by the scruff of its neck.

Felice gave a sycophantic smile and exited, holding the cat firmly to her bosom.

The maid marched upstairs to the bedchamber where a fire was burning brightly. The room was as clean as a new pin. A shame to sully it with paw marks and hair.

Felice crossed to the window and tugged at the latch with one hand, holding firmly onto Peter who gave a *miaow* of protest. The window swung open, letting in a flurry of snow. Felice threw the cat as far as she could, slammed the window, and set about mopping up the traces of melting snow from the floor.

"That's that," thought the maid, feeling more cheerful. "Good-bye cat! I will say it ran off."

But Felice felt less cheerful when her mistress entered the bedchamber, some ten minutes later, carrying a small dish of chopped liver.

"Peter!" said my lady. "Only look what I have for you. Here, puss, puss, puss!"

Felice compressed her lips and turned down the bedcovers.

"Where is the cat?" demanded Emily sharply.

"I do not know, my lady," said the maid, without turning around. "Perhaps he go away."

"Perhaps nothing," snapped Emily. "What have you done with him?"

"Me? But nothing, I assure you, my lady."

Emily got down on her hands and knees and searched under the bed and under the furniture. She found the still damp, recently cleaned patch under the window.

"What's this, Felice?" she cried. "Did you open the window?"

"As God is my witness," said the maid, folding her hands over the black silk of her gown and turning her eyes up so that the whites showed.

"I don't believe you," said Emily. "You wicked, wicked girl. You *smell* of guilt."

Emily ran out of the room and down the stairs. The noise from the dining room was very cheerful and jolly. The servants were obviously relaxing, enjoying their own company. Emily hesitated, her hand on the door of the dining room. To summon the exhausted servants to help her look for a mere kitten would be a disgraceful thing to do. She simply must try to find Peter on her own. With a little sigh, she put the hood of her cloak up about her head, and, wrapping herself firmly in its folds, she let herself out of the inn into the howling white wilderness outside.

The Earl of Devenham arrived some fifteen minutes later in a very bad temper indeed. He had lost his way in the storm several times. He was frozen to the bone. The landlord assured him that my lady was well, and this only added fuel to the earl's temper. To have risked the life of himself and his groom, not to mention the lives of two prime pieces of horseflesh to rescue a silly girl who did not need rescuing, was enough to try the patience of a saint.

He did not immediately go into the inn, having been assured of his wife's safety by the landlord, who had come outside to welcome him; instead, he went around to the stables to attend to his horse.

After he had rubbed down his horse and given it fodder and had seen it wrapped in a warm blanket that had been heated before the tack-room fire, the earl was feeling hungry and drowsy.

He decided to see Emily first. Would he kiss her? Perhaps he just might.

But the only person waiting in my lady's bed-chamber was the maid, Felice.

"Where is your mistress?" demanded the earl.

"My lady go out."

"*Go out?* Go out where?"

"She . . . I mean, my lady have this little cat and she think it go out in the storm and so she go out."

"And you let your mistress go out in this storm alone?"

The maid spread her hands in a peculiarly Gallic gesture, absolving herself of responsibility or blame.

The earl strode back down the stairs and called loudly for his servants. "Not you, John," he said to his exhausted Swiss. "The rest of you, my lady is somewhere outside looking for a *cat.* I do not like to send you all out in the snow again, but you must help me in the search. She cannot have gone very far. You wait here," he told John the coachman, "and tell the landlord he must send his own serv-ants to hunt for her as well. Do not bunch together. We will go in different directions."

The earl plunged into the storm, noticing as he did so that the visibility was becoming better, al-though the wind still howled.

"Is this going to be the pattern of my days?" he wondered savagely. "Running around in the worst weather this country has to offer, trying to find a runaway wife?"

He called and shouted into the storm. If she had any sense, so he thought, she would keep close to the inn. A cat would not go very far from warmth on such a night.

But Emily had no sense, so he assumed she had

probably plunged out of the inn yard and into the road.

He was stumbling waist-high into the road when the storm, with a great roar, left, as quickly as it had come. One minute he could hardly see a thing, and the next all was empty and white, stretching for miles.

He saw, in the distance, a small black dot against the snow and, shouting *Emily* at the top of his voice, struggled toward it.

One minute she was so very far away. The next she was tottering forward into his arms.

He held her very close and then turned up her face and kissed her mouth, feeling her cold, frozen lips turn warm under the pressure of his own. The world became a magic place, a white plain of passion, where they seemed to turn and turn and turn in each other's arms in slow, lingering ecstasy.

Then she drew back and sighed, "Oh, Peter," and he could have struck her to the ground. He had assumed there were no loves in her past. Who was this Peter whose name she cried after that long and passionate kiss?

Emily looked wonderingly up into his stern, angry face. His eyes were as cold as the landscape.

"I am very glad to see you, Peregrine," she said timidly. "I came out to look for my cat."

"Then I take leave to inform you that you have put me and my exhausted servants to a great deal of worry and unnecessary trouble. A cat will not go far from food and warmth. You should have searched about the inn. Pray return immediately and forget about the wretched animal."

"I cannot," wailed Emily, tears beginning to run down her face. "He is so small and . . ."

"God give me patience," the earl said between his teeth. "Let me carry you, and you can tell me about the cursed beast. Now, when did you last see the brute?"

"Felice took him up to our bedchamber, and, when I arrived, the cat was gone, and there was a damp spot on the floor under the window, although Felice swore she had not opened it. . . ."

"She opened it," he interrupted, "and threw the cat out, which is what any servant in her right mind would do. You should have searched in the snowdrifts under the window."

"Oh, do hurry," begged Emily. "Even now he may be dead."

"With luck," muttered the earl. Once more, he found himself carrying her back to the inn. A great black wave of depression hit him. Not only was Mary Anstey in love with another man; now it seemed as if his wife were mourning for some fellow called Peter.

He set her down in the inn yard after calling out to the servants that she had been found. "I want to make one thing very plain, my lady," he said. "This precious cat, if you want to keep it, goes straight to the stables. The bedchamber is nowhere for a cat."

"It is only a kitten, Devenham," pleaded Emily. "Which is the bedroom, so that I may search underneath the window?"

The earl strode off to question the landlord. "The west side," he called. Emily ran after him, tripping and stumbling through the drifts of snow.

She followed in the earl's footsteps around the side of the inn. The earl was already bending over, digging with his bare hands in the snow.

At last, he gave a yelp and withdrew his hand. "I believe I have found your cat, madam," he said coldly, showing her a long, bleeding scratch across the back.

"Let me," said Emily eagerly. She gently brushed away the snow until a little cave was revealed, and, in the cave, one small, cold, angry kitten.

"Oh, *Peter!*" cried Emily, laughing. "I was so worried. My poor, poor Peter." The kitten purred and snuggled up under her chin.

"Peter?" said the earl sharply. "why do you call the cat Peter? After someone?"

"No." Emily laughed. "The only Peter I know is Peter Cummings. I called him Peter because he's like a little rock. Very brave, are you not, my darling."

The earl felt suddenly quite lightheaded. "Well, bring Peter into the inn," he said. He felt he loved the world, he felt he could even bear the cat.

"Good Peter." The earl laughed, reaching out a hand to the cat. The cat seized his thumb and bit it.

"Oh, I am sorry," said Emily anxiously. "He did not bite you very hard, I trust. You see, he is very young and playful."

"I think that animal is possessed by the devil," said the earl, glaring at the cat, who glared back.

"But let us get indoors. I have had enough of this snow to last me a lifetime."

After the earl had eaten a hearty supper, he went upstairs to the bedroom, to find his wife asleep. He had not told her that he had not ordered a separate room for himself. He sat on the edge of the bed and studied her sleeping face. Well, no one could call Emily missish, he thought. She seemed able to go through the most dreadful weather without even catching a chill. She looked very young and inno-cent with her gold hair streaming out across the pillow. He must go easy with her, he decided. Per-haps if he wooed her gently, he might find a pas-sionate and loving wife like the Emily he had held in his arms out in the snow. He must make her *want* to come to his bed.

He undressed and slipped between the sheets. He turned on his side to blow out the bed candle, and five sharp little claws sank through his nightshirt, into his bottom.

"What the deuce!" The earl leaped from the bed and ripped back the sheets, while Emily mumbled and protested in her sleep. A small bundle of raised fur and glaring green eyes challenged him from the middle of the bed.

"Oh, no, my friend," said the earl softly. "I am not going to have a mangy cat as a rival." He scooped the cat up with one quick movement and placed it on the floor. "I must ask Emily not to be too harsh with Felice," he thought sleepily. "It is an eminently throwable cat."

Mary's council of war did not go as she had expected. Mr. and Mrs. Anstey said she was making a to-do about nothing. Yes, Mary could throw herself away on Mr. Cummings if she wished, but that was no reason why Mary should be jealous of Emily's being such a great countess. In vain did Mary and Mr. Cummings plead that Emily was unhappy. Mr. and Mrs. Anstey refused to listen. Mr. Cummings shrewdly realized that if he continued to protest, then perhaps his chances of marrying Mary would diminish again, and so he signaled to his love to be silent and confided to her in the hall, when the door was closed on Mr. and Mrs. Anstey, that it would be more politic to try again on the morrow.

For three days the snow kept the Anstey family housebound. But on the fourth day, when the roads were once again clear, Mary received allies from an unexpected quarter. Sir James and Lady Harrison, together with their ill-favored son, Billy, came to call.

The Harrisons, Mary was well aware, had suffered much from Emily's grand manner, so she set herself to please, wondering all the while why the Harrisons looked so *triumphant*.

"You will be visiting your daughter soon?" said Lady Harrison, exchanging a sly look with her husband. "She will no doubt be in sore need of your help."

"Why?" asked Mrs. Anstey, fat face agoggle. "Our Emily is so taken up with being a countess and all, it will be a bit before she has time for her old parents. Ah, yes, she's gone far above us *all*," added Mrs. Anstey, with a malicious look at Lady Harrison.

Billy Harrison was slouched in his chair, picking at his teeth with a goose quill and making ugly sucking noises. He affected the Corinthian mode of dress, or what he fondly thought was the Corinthian mode, a belcher handkerchief tied round his throat instead of a cravat, and a great many whip points thrust in his buttonhole. His boots were muddy and his leather breeches creaked every time he shifted his bulk in his chair.

"Ah, poor dear Emily," sighed Lady Harrison, applying a wisp of handkerchief to one dry eye. "I was just saying to Mr. Cummings this morning that all one can do is pray."

Mr. Anstey sat bolt upright. "Speak plain, my lady," he said. "Is there something about our Emily you know that we don't?"

Lady Harrison gave a genteel cough. "Really, I don't know quite how to begin."

Billy Harrison removed the quill from his mouth and grinned. " 'S all over London," he said. "Devenham's been seen everywhere with his ladylove, Cordelia Haddington. Was with her all over Christmas. Told her he was tricked into marrying Emily and he wishes he were out o' it."

Mary turned quite white. "I do not believe a word of this," she cried. "Malicious gossip."

"My dear," said Lady Harrison, leaning forward and giving Mary's hand a squeeze. "Your loyalty does you credit. But, ah me, what Billy says is the way of it. It's the talk of the town."

Mrs. Anstey struggled for composure. "We'll find it's all a hum," she said comfortably. "My lord would not cheat on a girl he had just wed."

"Unless he thought *himself* cheated," said Sir

James with a great horse laugh. "He was supposed to marry Mary, wasn't he? Aye, and why was Emily, if she was supposed to be the one he was marrying, wearing a brown wig in church, heh?"

"I have never heard of such rubbish," said Mary hotly. "My sister is very happily married. I am surprised, nay *shocked*, to find you the bearers of such malicious gossip."

"I am sure it was well meant," said Mrs. Anstey, unable to believe that her ascendancy over the Harrisons was crumbling.

Lady Harrison stood up and shook out her skirts. "It was merely told to you in friendship, Miss Anstey," she said. "That Cordelia Haddington—who goes everywhere although she is not exactly *comme il faut*—is telling the world and his wife that Devenham means to have the marriage annulled."

After the Harrisons had left, Mary rounded up her parents. "*Now* will you listen to me," she said. "I told you and *told* you that Emily was monstrous unhappy, that Emily said there was another woman in the case. If I believed Devenham meant to have the marriage annulled, I would not *care*. But it is Emily I am thinking of. Are you going to set social ambition above your daughter's happiness?"

"No," said Mr. Anstey, after a long silence. "It is strange, but I always thought that once I had the county eating out of my hand, so to speak, I would be a happy man. But I ain't. I prefer the city merchants and their wives, and that's a fact. And so do you, my love," he said to his wife. "You ain't enjoyed it one bit. Oh, it was fun when Emily put them all in their place, but you did say yourself you thought Emily was sad or she would never have behaved so. We've done wrong by our daughter and we must right it. If Devenham has not already taken steps to have the marriage annulled, then we must persuade him to do so. And we must go to this Maxton Court so that we can tell Emily there's nothing to be ashamed of. She can come back and forget she ever was a countess.

"You know, all these years we've stayed here, I've been bored to flinders. I want to get back to the city where I know my friends. I want to sit down in a chophouse and feel at ease without some jumped-up gentry sneering about trade."

"Let us leave for Maxton Court as soon as possible," begged Mary.

"We'll need to wait until the roads clear, my love," said Mr. Anstey. "Cheer up, mother," he said to his wife. "You'll get used to the idea of being plain Mrs. Nobody of Nowhere soon enough."

"No, I won't," sobbed Mrs. Anstey. "I was that proud of having a countess for a daughter."

Mary and Mr. Anstey tried to persuade her of the vanity of clinging to mere titles, but Mrs. Anstey wept on and would not be comforted.

To Mary's dismay, Mr. Anstey had changed his tune by the following morning. He was once more the Mr. Anstey who had sent penniless young Captain Tracey to the rightabout and yet had welcomed home the rich Earl of Devenham without a blush.

It seemed that people changed their characters in a day only in novels and in Haymarket dramas. Winter began to give way to spring, with mist ris-

113

ing from the brown fields in the evening and birds chirping in the hedgerows in the morning, and still the Ansteys remained at Malden Grand. Emily's cheerful letters were no help to Mary, who thought she saw hidden misery and sadness beneath every line.

Mary had quite given up hope, when, one day late in March, Mr. and Mrs. Anstey arrived from their round of calls in great distress. The Harrisons had been entertaining their grand London friends, and, to the Ansteys' horror, Lady Harrison had urged those friends to impress on the Ansteys the peril in which their daughter's marriage stood. The friends, being lightweight, gossiping flibbertigibbets, were not loath to telling all and throwing in a great deal of fancy embroidery, besides. The result was that Mr. and Mrs. Anstey had reeled from the Harrisons' mansion, finally persuaded that their daughter was in the hands of a lustful, rakish monster who had every intention of ruining her and casting her out in the kennel.

After much debate, they decided to inform the earl of their impending arrival, and it was just as well they did. After a week's impatient wait, a letter came back from the earl's steward to say that my lord and lady had gone to London.

"London!" said Mr. Anstey. "Poor Emily. She will find out for herself. We must be on hand to comfort her."

"Let us leave immediately," said Mrs. Anstey, ever hopeful. "It may be all a hum. It is best to see for ourselves."

Mr. Anstey recalled a merchant friend who was leaving for the Indies and who would be glad to lease them his home in Russell Square. Not the most fashionable address, but then Mr. Anstey was weary of being fashionable.

Mary bid a fond farewell to Mr. Cummings, and the Ansteys set out.

If this lustful earl had kept his lusts outside his marriage and if Emily were still pure, the annulment of the marriage should be very easy.

Emily could consider herself well out of it. Mr. Anstey privately thought that any man who could live in celibacy with a beautiful young bride was strangely depraved.

But he did not voice his thoughts.

Chapter Eight

It was the cat who had ruined the pleasure of setting out for London.

My lord had been adamant. The cat had to stay behind at Maxton Court.

If Emily did not want to leave the cat, then Emily could stay as well.

Emily was in a state of misery. Relations between herself and her husband had slowly improved. Although he had not kissed her again, he had been charming and friendly. Gradually, they began to ride out together and talk in the evening until the candles burned low in their sockets. Both of them were enthusiastic about the new improvements to the estates.

The earl often kissed her hand when he said good night, and there was an increasing warmth in his eyes when he looked at her. But he still spent a great deal of the day on his own business or hunting with the local farmers or shooting with friends, and Emily was often left for long hours to her own devices. When the weather was too bad to make calls, she contented herself by playing in the Long Gallery with the cat, Peter, while the portraits of the haughty Devenhams looked down in surprise.

Emily often had to admit to herself that Peter had not exactly grown up into a handsome cat. He had grown very large, muscular, and heavy. His fur gleamed with health, but his fixed stare and torn ear gave him a sinister look.

He was devoted to her and tried to show his devotion by laying dead mice, voles, and other horrible trophies at her feet. But he had developed a nasty sense of humor, and it seemed as if his favorite sport had become earl-baiting. He loved to lie along ledges and the tops of wardrobes and wait for the earl to pass underneath, at which point he would lean down and swipe the earl with one paw.

Perhaps the earl would have allowed Peter to travel to London, for he was secretly amused at the horrible creature's devotion to Emily, but two days before they were to depart, Peter committed the worst crime of all.

The earl had decided to go into his wife's bedroom to say good night as part of his campaign plan. He had noticed the way Emily's eyes had begun to glow whenever she looked at him, but he still did not plan to rush his courtship. He was content to wait and take things one step at a time.

Emily looked very pretty sitting up in bed, reading a book, her golden curls covered by a frivolous lacy nightcap.

"Why . . . Peregrine!" exclaimed Emily. "Is anything the matter?"

"It is rather odd, don't you think," smiled the earl, coming to sit beside her on the bed, "when a man cannot enter his wife's bedroom without that wife thinking something is wrong."

"Oh, no . . . it's only . . . well, this is the first time."

"Don't look so alarmed," said the earl. "I am merely here to give you a good-night kiss."

Emily blushed rosily.

There was a soft thud as the large cat leaped on the bed. Its fur slowly rose and it green eyes glared.

All of a sudden, the earl lost his temper. A male rival was one thing, but he was damned if he was going to compete with a cat.

He seized Peter by the scruff of the neck, carried him to the door, hurled him out into the corridor, and returned to his wife.

"Now," he said, "where was I?"

He leaned over her. A miserable yowl rose from the passageway.

"Oh, Devenham," said Emily. "The poor animal."

"You had begun to call me Peregrine."

Yowl, yowl, *yowl.*

"He is only a cat, Peregrine. You mustn't treat him so badly."

"My lady, I am here to kiss you good night. Does that mean nothing to you?"

Emily smiled up at him and held out her arms. His lips had nearly reached hers when there came the sound of a heavy body throwing itself against the door.

Emily winced. Her lips were cold and chaste.

The earl drew back disappointed. Emily smiled

at him tremulously, knowing she had failed him, but what else could she do? The yowls were increasing along with the desperate thuds on the door.

"He'll knock his head senseless," she moaned.

The earl stood up. "I leave you to consider your ridiculous behavior, madam," he said stiffly. He stalked to the door and flung it open, and the cat hurtled into the room and straight onto the bed. The earl's lip curled in disgust as he went out and slammed the door.

But that was not the worst of it.

The following day, the earl had been helped into his clothes by his Swiss and had then noticed a speck among the snowy folds of his cravat.

He decided to find a new one and opened the drawer where the clean linen was kept. He was searching about for a length of cloth that was already starched when he became aware of the horrible smell arising from the drawer.

He rang the bell and stood rigid with fury until his Swiss came running in.

"Was that cat in here?" demanded the earl.

"Yes, my lord," said the servant. "Very amusing he is. He was watching me put away the clean linen, just like a human."

"Indeed. Well, when you turned your back, this is the result. Smell this."

The valet moved cautiously forward and then looked at his master in dismay.

"Exactly," said the earl grimly. "Cat's piss. Here and now I want it known that that animal is not to be allowed in my quarters or anywhere near my person."

Emily found the resulting scene blistering and painful. The end result was that Peter was to be taken out to the stables and left there until her return.

And so, instead of setting out cheerfully with her husband to London, a bit of Emily's heart was left behind in the stables. The fact was that Emily was sure of the cat's love. She was not at all sure of her husband's. She still sensed a woman somewhere in the background of his life in which she had no part. She was ashamed of her own fears and the timidity that kept her from her husband's bed. She felt the earl was waiting for her to make the first move rather than be humiliated by her rejection. But every time she thought of making that move, her fears returned to plague her.

Sometimes, Emily fervently wished she had driven on and left Peter to his own fate in the ditch.

She had gone to the stables to say a tearful farewell to the animal and although the head groom had assured her the cat would be well looked after and fed, she sensed an underlying contempt in his manner which she felt boded no good for the hapless Peter.

She was waiting in the carriage for her husband to join her. Their relations were still strained.

But it was with a queer lightening of her heart that she saw the smile on his face as he climbed into the carriage to join her. He stooped and kissed her warmly and quickly on the mouth, and she gave him an enchanting smile. He sat down beside her and took her hand in his. Emily's heart soared, and they were several miles on the road before she even thought about the cat or wondered what was happening to it.

The cat was much nearer than she realized. Behind her, at the back of the carriage, crouched down at the feet of the footmen in the rumble, among the folds of the bearskin rugs which were piled at their feet in case my lord or my lady should require them, crouched Peter. He was terrified at first by the motion of the carriage, but, after a time, the heat from the rugs made him feel drowsy. His eyes closed and he slept.

The posting inn lay some twenty miles from London in a market town called Shapphards. It was a spacious, pretty inn, built in the modern style with a porticoed entrance and a blue-and-gold coffee room, with a brass and walnut tap downstairs and well-appointed bedrooms with private parlors above.

Emily told herself she was glad her husband had taken a separate bedroom and fought down that niggling little wish that he would by *forcing* her to join him in his bed beat down her timidity. It would all be so simple, Emily felt, if he would kiss her and go on kissing her.

He looked splendidly formal with the diamond pin she had given him blazing among the snowy folds of his cravat. The parlor in which they sat down to dinner was light and charming, with a small bright fire, oak furniture, and pastel walls of nile green. The food was savory, and both fell to with a good appetite. When the servants were dismissed, the earl drew a small black box from his pocket and passed it to Emily. "For you, my sweet-ing."

Emily colored slightly at the endearment and opened the box.

An emerald, as green as spring grass, as green as Peter's eyes, flashed up at her from its gold set-ting.

"It's a ring, Peregrine," said Emily. "It is very lovely."

"You never did get an engagement ring, Emi-ly." He came around the table and lifted the ring. Her hand trembled slightly as he put it on her fin-ger. He raised her hand and kissed it.

Her eyes, lifted to his, were soft and brown, with little flecks of gold. Her lips were pink and beau-tifully shaped. Her . . .

"It reminds me of Peter's eyes," said Emily, turning the ring so that the green fire flashed in the candlelight.

The earl made a sound like *gerrumph* and stalked back to his seat. Emily looked at him nerv-ously and cursed her unruly tongue. She longed to say something light and warm and affectionate. If only she had the courage to tell the truth, to face this husband of hers and say: I want to love you, I think I could love you, but you scare me to death. Please help me.

But instead, she said, "I cannot help worrying about the cat. Will they be kind to it, do you think?"

The earl poured himself a glass of wine and said in measured tones, "They have instructions to take care of the animal. They are not in the way of being disobedient or they would not be in my employ.

They will treat the cat more like the animal it is and less like a lover."

"You are jealous," said Emily, "of a cat." And inside her head, a voice was screaming at her to behave herself.

"I have no reason to be jealous," he said with a shrug. "Only men in love are jealous."

Emily winced.

Well, sneered her inner voice, what did you expect? He gives you a beautiful ring and kisses your hand, and all you can do, instead of saying thank you, is to worry about a horrible cat with a torn ear.

"The reason I am justifiably annoyed," the earl went on, "is because you did not pause to thank me for the ring."

"Thank you, Devenham."

"Too late. Have you finished? Then perhaps you would like to retire and leave me to the more pleasant company of this decanter of port. It provides solace and comfort when nothing else is offered."

For one split second, Emily was on the point of begging his forgiveness. But he looked so hard, so unyielding; and then there was always that feeling about him, that *emanation* from him of the presence of another woman.

"Do not worry," she said, rising to her feet, "we will soon be in London and you can return to the arms of your mistress."

The slight flicker of surprise in his eyes made her own suddenly fill with tears, and she walked quickly from the room and slammed the door behind her.

The deuce! thought the earl bitterly. Some scandalmonger has told her.

Emily entered her bedroom, too angry to cry. So there *was* a mistress. The expression in his eyes had given him away. She was glad, glad, *glad* she had not encouraged his advances, not allowed his *nasty*, soiled, *used* body anywhere near her own. She was shaking with rage, incensed with rage; her whole being was sour with a rampant jealousy as green as the ring on her finger.

Miaow! Emily jumped in the air with fright and then stared at the bed, unable to believe her eyes.

Stretched out on the counterpane was the cat, Peter.

At the same moment, she heard the maid Felice's light step in the passageway outside.

Emily ran forward and grabbed the cat, bundled him into the wardrobe, and slammed the door. She was leaning with her back against the door when the maid came into the room.

"I will not need you tonight," said Emily. "I will undress myself."

Yowl.

The maid stared at Emily, who put her hands over her face and yowled a fairly good imitation of the cat. "I-I am sore distressed, F-Felice," she wailed. "Go quickly."

"Yes, my lady," came the maid's anxious voice. "First, let me find my lady's night rail and turn down the covers and . . ."

Yowl went the cat, and yowl, yowl, *yowl* went Emily. Felice knew of the ban on Peter. Emily was terrified that if the maid found out about the cat, she would immediately go to Devenham.

"Go away," screamed Emily.

Felice fled. With a sigh of relief, Emily opened the wardrobe door.

"Poor Peter," she said, picking up the cat and carrying it to the bed. "Poor, poor Peter."

She stroked the cat's fur and talked nonsense to it while it purred loudly and bumped its large head, with the ragged ear, against her chin.

"How on earth did you manage to travel this far? At least he will not try to see me tonight, Peter," said Emily, setting the cat down on the floor. "He is much, much too angry with me."

She began to take off her clothes and prepare for bed.

Felice was a very worried servant. That her mistress was in a demented state was all too painfully obvious. A good servant should not interfere in the affairs of her mistress and master. But what if my lady was yowling in that odd way because she was ill? And what if the earl found out that Felice had been negligent in her duty by leaving my lady alone?

Felice was very much afraid of the Earl of Devenham.

She was halfway down the stairs leading from Emily's room, standing on the landing, when the earl's Swiss came up with an armful of freshly starched cravats.

Felice liked the Swiss, who was called John Phillips. His real name was Jean-Philippe Danton, but he had anglicized his name long before entering the earl's service. He was from the Canton Vaud, so Felice was able to lapse into her native tongue. In muscular strength he did not compare well with the second footman, being a wiry little man with a sallow face and a quizzical expression, but Felice had become as fond of him as she could be of anybody she was not exactly in love with. Talking in French, she told him of the scene just enacted by Emily.

"You must go and see my lord," counseled John. "He is drinking wine in the parlor. My lady could have the vapors."

With Gallic bluntness, Felice pointed out it was not the time of the month for my lady to have the vapors, but, with a little shrug, agreed she should say something to the master.

The fact that the earl looked singularly grim and forbidding did not deter Felice, who thought it was any proper aristocrat's place to look stern and forbidding.

She promptly launched into a dramatic description of Emily's distress.

"Thank you," said the earl, when she had finished. "You may go. You did well to tell me. I will go to Lady Devenham immediately."

With a pleasant feeling of duty well done, Felice went downstairs to the kitchens to make herself some tea and to gossip with the inn servants, and the earl went to his wife's room. The door was locked.

He knocked on it until he heard Emily call out, "Who's there?"

"It is I, Peregrine," he called. "Felice tells me you are upset."

Inside the room, Emily looked at the cat and the cat looked at Emily. At the sound of the earl's voice, its fur had started to rise.

"I am very well now," called Emily. "I had the headache."

"Open the door."

Emily had always wondered what wringing the hands meant. Now she knew.

If Devenham found the cat, he would divorce her, or beat her, or kill her. If she put the animal in the wardrobe, it would simply yowl and cry, and she did not think the earl would be as easily fooled as Felice.

Made bold by desperation, she called, "Go to your room, my love. I will join you there in a moment."

There was silence while she waited with beating heart.

Then the earl's voice, surprised and amused, said from outside the door, "Very well, my sweeting. Do not keep me waiting long."

His footsteps retreated.

"There!" hissed Emily at the cat. "You useless lump of carriage rug. I am going to lose my virginity so that he does not wring *both* our necks."

Feeling like a French aristocrat about to go to the scaffold, Emily picked up a candle in its flat stick and hurried along the corridor in the direction of her husband's room. In her fright and anxiety, she forgot to pull her own door securely behind her.

She pushed open the door of the earl's room. He was in his nightshirt.

Gracious, thought Emily, the man must have *torn* his clothes off to get undressed so quickly. Then she thought it strange that a man dressed in a white nightshirt with a great deal of lace about the throat and wrists should manage to look so

127

compellingly masculine. The black hair that met in that widow's peak and those thin black eyebrows over the flat silver eyes gave him a satanic look.

His mouth curved in a sweet smile, and all at once, Emily felt that everything was going to be all right and that perhaps she should be grateful to the wretched cat for making her take the necessary step.

He held out his arms, and Emily walked into them and buried her head against his chest, feeling the heat from his body and the steady thud of his heart against her cheek.

He lifted her gently in his arms, carried her to the bed, and laid her down. He stretched out beside her and took her in his arms again. It was very odd, thought Emily, that they were lying on top of the covers. Surely, one went underneath to perform all those dark and sinister midnight deeds. And he had left the candles burning!

He gathered her to him and pressed her body against his own. He kissed her eyelids, the curve of her jaw, and the tip of her nose. She could feel her breasts swelling and hardening and hoped idiotically that this was all natural and that they were supposed to do that. She noticed he smelled faintly of wine and lavender water and soap. His lips gently covered her own, and she forgot about everything else. Or nearly.

Just as her body felt as if it were melting and fusing into his own, just when her lips were parting under his, just when the sweet surging, bittersweet pain in the pit of her stomach was about to lead her to crave further intimacy, there came a soft thud at the door.

Low down on the door.

Peter.

Emily suddenly went rigid in the earl's arms, waiting for that first telltale yowl.

Abruptly, the earl freed his mouth and propped himself up on one elbow. "What is the matter, my love?" he asked, his voice husky, seductive.

Thud.

Emily cringed, but the earl had heard nothing—yet—and was waiting for her answer.

Poor Emily thought of his rage and fury if he found the cat outside. She did not realize that if she had only surrendered to him, then he would have let her have a whole zoo.

"I *can't*."

She wrenched herself from his arms and his bed and hurtled out of the room, clad only in her flimsy nightgown. She tripped headlong over the cat, scrambled to her feet again, grabbed the animal, and ran to her own room, slammed the door behind her, and locked it.

What am I to do? thought Emily. Oh, poor Peregrine. He will hate me forever.

"I *hate you*," she said to the cat who was now purring ecstatically on the bed, prancing up and down and digging its claws into the quilt.

Then Emily's eye fell on the little jug of milk on the tea tray. She poured some into a saucer and carefully added a few drops of laudanum.

The cat eagerly lapped up the milk, finished it, stretched, and began to wash itself in front of the fire, while Emily fretted and waited and tried to will it to go to sleep.

"I dare not give the beast any more," she said aloud, "or it might die."

Meanwhile, the Earl of Devenham had bitten the pillow, punched the wall, drunk half a bottle of brandy, and taken himself out to the back yard of the inn, where he doused himself under the pump.

Wet, cold, demoralized, and weary, he climbed the stairs to his room.

Emily was standing in the middle of his room, waiting for him. The cat had gone to sleep at last.

"Peregrine," she said softly and held out her arms.

The earl gave her one horrified look. "I have had more than a man can stand this evening, madam," he grated. He marched her to the door, pushed her out into the corridor, and locked the door behind her.

Emily returned to her own room and cried herself to sleep.

In the morning, she wearily dragged herself from bed, punched air-holes in a bandbox, and stuffed the drugged and heavy cat inside. The earl breakfasted in his room.

Silently, they climbed into the carriage together. Emily put the bandbox with the cat on the seat opposite and placed her jewel box and another bandbox next to it as a sort of camouflage.

The earl said not a word. He seemed once more master of himself and his emotions—"faultily faultless, icily regular, splendidly null."

He looked every inch the perfect English aristocrat. His calm dead face seemed to say: "These are my carriage, my servants, my wife," in that order.

His heavy eyelids drooped and he fell asleep before the inn was out of sight.

He awoke on the outskirts of London. Emily cheerfully commented on the weather—cold—the suburbs—quaint—and the state of the nation—confused, to which he replied, "Indeed, odso," and "really," until she lapsed into uneasy silence.

They were nearing his town house in Clarence Square in the West End of London, when the bandbox lid began to move. Too frightened to do or say anything, Emily sat as if turned to stone.

A large, furry head poked out, and one green eye surveyed the Earl of Devenham and his stricken lady.

"I am glad you will have company in London, my lady," said the Earl of Devenham, looking at the cat, "for you will have little of mine."

Chapter Nine

London was different from the London Emily had known. The West End was a world away from the bustle and commerce of the city. At first, there seemed to be a certain monotony in the view: the pavements wide and smooth; every door with its stone steps, its iron railing, and its lamp; each house exactly the same as its neighbor, except for the number on the door and the name of the occupant. At night, the straightness of the streets was made more so by a long line of lamps set out in regular order.

Even the dusty squares were set about with buildings, as neatly as a child's toy, facing a railinged square of cropped trees, cropped bushes, and cropped grass.

Any hope of spring seemed to have died. The days were cloudy and foggy, of a uniform gray. Sometimes a ray of sun would pierce the perpetual mist, making it float at the end of the streets, bathed in a golden hue, but all too soon the brief light would be extinguished as the fog rolled across the sun again.

The air was loaded with small flakes of soot, a sort of sooty snow, which fell gently on the clothes of the fashionable, sticking to clothes and linen. Under its modern title of influenza, the malady the French called catch-cold had recently swept London.

The Thames did not divide London as the Seine did Paris, that is, with half of the city on one side and half on the other. The other side of the Thames, that is, the Surrey side, was only an extensive suburb dotted with depressing warehouses and manufactories.

Emily thought that London, had she been able to fly above it, would present a patchy black and white appearance, like the hide of some huge, sleeping animal. The buildings were mainly constructed of Portland stone. Smoke blackened the white walls, and the rain washed only certain parts of them. Here there would be a whole column as white as chalk, and there, its neighbor, as black as the soot which darkened it.

It was in the evening, when what little light there was began to fade, that London became a magic place with carriages rolling over the cobbles and houses ablaze with lights. Then the shops came into their own, with many thousands of candles lighting up silverware, engravings, books, clocks, glass, pewter, paintings, women's finery, gold and precious stones, and endless coffee houses and lottery offices. Each street looked as if it were lit up for a fair. The apothecaries harlequinned the streets with the light from their display glasses filled with spirits, purple, yellow, and verdigris-green. Most dazzling of all were the confectioners with their candelabra and their hanging festoons and Spanish grapes and pineapples, their pyramids of apples and oranges, their rich cakes and tarts, all served by exceptionally pretty girls with silk caps and white arms.

And the noise! The din, clatter, and hum of thousands of tongues, the clamor of bells in the church towers, the postmen, organs, fiddles, the hurdy-gurdies of the mountebanks, and the cries from the street vendors selling hot and cold food.

To Felice, it was an unending delight, and Emily sometimes went on shopping expeditions only to buy things she did not want, in order to lighten the burden of her own misery in watching the maid's enjoyment.

The earl was hardly ever at home. Emily received callers and invitations but was too timid to venture out on her own, so the stiff gold cards piled up on the mantelpiece, invitations to balls and routs and theaters, all to be answered with a polite excuse.

There were the perpetual beaux, all too ready to attach themselves to a pretty, married lady with an absent husband, but Emily hardly noticed any of them.

She contented herself by reading, sewing, and talking to the cat. Sometimes she loved the cat and sometimes she hated it. That was the trouble with cats. They often had an almost human reaction to things, whereas dogs were uncomplicated, jolly, undemanding, and affectionate.

"I will sell you and buy a dog," Emily would threaten, and Peter would flatten his ears, lash his tail, and then begin to purr, for he did not believe a word of it.

The earl had paid calls on the fair Cordelia, but he could not bring himself to be intimate with her again. He was aware she had gossiped excessively, and that set her down in his eyes to the ranks of the Fashionable Impure. Unaware of his change of heart and thinking he was being discreet because of his wife's presence in town, Cordelia continued to hope for his divorce and the subsequent marriage to herself.

At last, a warm spring wind blew the fog to shreds. A pale, duck-egg blue sky stretched over London, and young leaves fluttered bravely from the branches of trees in the park.

The earl was riding with his friend, Arthur Chester, on this first fine day. He could not quite remember why he had suggested coming to London in the first place and was longing to return to the country to see things grow.

After an energetic gallop, they reined in under an oak and dismounted, strolling over the new, springy grass.

"You know," said Mr. Chester, "it do seem odd, though I don't suppose I should mention it."

"Then don't," said the earl, barely listening. He had all at once remembered that the night when Emily had spurned his love-making had been the very night when she had revealed she had heard of Cordelia.

"Well, it is damned odd," pursued Mr. Chester. "Gettin' to be the talk of the town, and the Season ain't even begun. Beginning to say you're a sort of bluebeard."

"What?" The earl's head jerked round.

"Well, Lady Devenham don't *go* anywhere. Jerry Banks was telling everyone he took her flowers and a book the other day. Said it was fit to break a man's heart, all that wonderful beauty hidden away."

The earl frowned. His first thought was one of amazement that Emily was actually considered beautiful. He thought her beautiful by country standards, but then he had grown accustomed to her appearance.

"And young Guy Fox sent her a poem, but she didn't really like it. Must have been a bit warm, for she returned it with a little note saying she felt the sentiments were too strong and, as your wife, she could not accept the poem.

"And Jack Delancey . . ."

"*Now* you are talking about strong meat. Delancey's the worst rake in town."

Mr. Chester poked at the turf with his whip. "'S matter of fact," he said cautiously, "that's what they're saying about *you*."

"I give them no reason."

"Cordelia talked fit to beat the band."

"Useless gossip."

"She wouldn't have had anything to gossip about had you not gossiped to *her*."

The earl flushed. He could not believe that he was the one who was wrong. He had behaved nobly. He had gone ahead with the marriage. He had not forced his attentions on her. All he had done was

. . . hold her up to ridicule? Damn Cordelia! Her tongue was as loose as her . . . never mind.

"As a matter of fact," said the earl, striving to introduce a light note into the guilt-ridden atmosphere, "I do have a rival for my wife's affections. Peter. She's in bed with him every night, stroking and caressing him."

"You amaze me. I don't believe a word of it. Why, Lady Devenham is an angel. The sweetest, purest lady of the ton."

"I was merely joking," said the earl mildly. "I was referring to her cat. But I did not know you had been calling on my wife."

"Least I could do," muttered Mr. Chester. "Poor, lonely thing."

"May I remind you you are speaking about my *wife*."

"We all thought she was as good as wasn't," said Mr. Chester. "What with Cordelia blabbing about divorce and you being absent. Fellows are even whispering that Lady Devenham is a virgin."

"Enough!" cried the earl. "We will not discuss my wife any further, and you may spread the word that anyone else doing so will be asked to name his seconds."

He turned abruptly on his heel and strode off, leaving Mr. Chester looking sadly after him.

The earl was prey to the most terrible feelings of remorse. For all those long years in the army, he had disciplined his thoughts. He felt he had behaved wisely and fairly with the men in his command. The image of Mary Anstey waiting faithfully for him had kept him from the excesses of his fellow officers. He had been appalled to find, on his return, that his feelings for Mary were exactly nothing. He had not been able to believe it and had felt it was all the fault of the Ansteys for having sullied such a pure and tender love. It had been their fault that it had withered and died. Emily posing as her sister had seemed part and parcel of the Anstey behavior.

But you wanted her, his conscience nagged him. The truth is it was Emily Anstey you really wanted, but your pride would not let you admit it to yourself.

He shook his head as if to clear it. He felt like an old and depraved tyrant. No wonder she clung to that ridiculous animal. She was lonely.

It was midafternoon, and fashionable London was just cautiously beginning to poke its long nose out of doors.

He recalled guiltily that he had hardly spent any of the daylight hours in his own home. He had breakfasted at coffee houses, dined in pastry shops during the day, and then at one of his clubs in the evening, returning home only at dawn.

It was not too late to make amends, he thought. He felt such a tender rush of affection for his young wife as he strode into the hallway of his town house that, if she had come out to meet him, he would have kissed her on the spot.

He laid his hat and whip on the hall table and straightened his cravat in the looking glass.

With an unusual feeling of anticipation, he turned away from the looking glass to go in search of his wife.

Crash!

A vase sailed past his ear and shattered into fragments of red and gold on the floor.

He looked up.

Peter the cat looked smugly back from a ledge next to the glass. The earl extended a threatening hand, whereupon Peter sat up on his hind legs and batted at the hand with his paws.

It was at this point that Emily came running out, and the earl forgot all about his own guilt, about his warm feelings toward her, and glared down at her wide, startled eyes.

"That animal," he said, "has just smashed a Ming vase."

Emily signaled a footman to pick up the pieces. "It was not Ming, Devenham," she said mildly. "It was rather an awful thing that Lord Brockenham gave me. He made it himself. He was so proud of it. He *threw* it, you see. I put it on that ledge because Peter usually sits there, and I hoped the cat would knock it off so that I could tell Lord Brockenham in all honesty that the cat had broken it."

He watched her silently, and Emily felt nervous. He looked so stern. Actually, the earl was seeing his wife with new eyes, noticing the gold luster of her hair, the perfect bloom on her cheek, and the exquisitely trim figure shown to advantage by a morning gown of finest muslin. The he noticed the shadows under her eyes and felt a pang of compunction. He was about to apologize to her for his absences, when she said, "I must return to my callers, Devenham," so he contented himself by saying: "Then I shall join you."

His black brows snapped into a frown as he entered the room. There were at least six gentlemen, including that notorious rake, Jack Delancey. There were no ladies present.

He was so frigidly austere that he soon drove away the guests.

Emily felt a pain at her heart. It was useless trying to hang on to this marriage-in-name-only. Somehow, she must find courage to give him his freedom and send him on his way.

He flicked through the card rack and pulled out a silver-ornamented invitation. "I see Lord and Lady Foss are giving a ball," he said. "They have a vastly pretty villa in Kensington."

"It is tonight," said Emily timidly. "I sent a note of refusal."

"And what excuse did you give?"

"I said you were indisposed, Devenham."

"Perhaps I was," he said with a sudden laugh. "Would you still care to go?"

"Oh, Devenham, I have *never* been to a ton ball."

"Then I will send a footman to say we will be there."

"I haven't a ball gown grand enough, Devenham."

"That gown you are wearing is new. Surely you ordered something in the way of evening wear."

"Well, I did," said Emily timidly, "but when it transpired, as I thought that we were not to go anywhere, I cancelled it. Papa always said that, although we had money, we should not spend it uselessly." She hung her head.

"I am sure you can find something," he said anxiously, his voice slightly gruff. "Fetch your bonnet and call Felice. I know a dressmaker who will be able to find you something."

"Imagine you knowing dressmakers, Peregrine," said Emily with a gurgle of laughter. Then her laughter died, and a shadow crossed her face.

He put his hands on her shoulders and looked down at her bent head. "There is no other lady in my life . . . now, Emily," he said.

"But there was?" said Emily, raising her eyes, which glittered with tears.

"Yes, there was. But not any more. Do you trust me?"

"Oh, yes," said Emily, suddenly happy.

"Then get your bonnet," he said.

Mary Anstey and her parents sifted through the information they had collected on Emily's marriage and found it added up to disaster. "It's all about town," said Mr. Anstey gloomily. "Devenham don't want her."

"I think we should call," said Mary firmly. "All this cloak-and-dagger business is ridiculous, and it is all your idea, Mama. You keep clinging to the hope that Emily will remain Countess of Devenham."

"Divorce," wailed Mrs. Anstey. "The shame. The disgrace."

"I think our daughter's happiness must come before all else," said Mr. Anstey. "Mary has the right of it. We must simply go and ask Emily if she is happy. Our scouts say she never leaves the house in Clarence Square."

It was nine in the evening when the Anstey carriage rolled up to the Earl of Devenham's town house. Three dismayed faces looked at the butler when he announced my lord and my lady were not at home.

"We'll wait," said Mr. Anstey firmly.

Emily was in seventh heaven as she trotted happily along on the arm of her tall husband, with Felice and a footman following behind. Now the shops were magic places full of wonderful things. The London shopkeeper prided himself on the neatness of his shopfront. His little portico and the pillasters and cornices were imitations of Lydian, Serpentine, porphyry, and Verdes antique marble, and the shopkeepers who had the good fortune to serve any branch of the royal family immediately placed large sculptures of their several arms and supporters over their doors, and their own names and businesses in gold characters.

Wooden highlanders stood outside the snuff and tobacco shops, staring militantly, with painted eyes, at the fashionable throng.

"Our prince regent is much enamored of the highlander," ventured Emily, timidly trying out a little harmless piece of London gossip on her husband.

"His Royal Highness sometimes goes a little far." The earl laughed. "At a ball given by the Duchess of York for Princess Charlotte, Prinny caused quite a commotion. All of a sudden, in the middle of a dance, he heaved his huge bulk up from the couch and called for a Highland fling. Charlotte must be taught the steps, and he himself would teach her.

"A space was cleared in the center of the room for the regent to take the floor. With the princess dutifully following his capers, he pointed his toes, flung out his arms, and jigged and hopped, emitting Gaelic shrieks, until one more hop sent him sprawling.

"Charlotte, choking back her giggles, flew to his assistance. His gentlemen, preternaturally solemn, hoisted him up and bore him off to bed. Poor Prinny!"

Emily laughed delightedly, but more because her handsome husband was making an effort to entertain her than over amusement at the prince regent's discomfiture.

They stopped outside a jeweler's and looked at the trays of gems in the dim window. "Let me see your wedding ring," said the earl suddenly.

Emily twisted nervously at the heavy gold band. "It will not come off, Peregrine," she said. "Why do you want it?"

"I never had it inscribed," he said. "Put your glove on again. Perhaps another time. It is a sentimental notion. I thought of one of the old Jacobean rhymes, something pretty. Do not worry. I have no intention of emulating the Bishop of Salisbury."

"What did he do?" asked Emily, happy again, for she had had a sudden stab of fear that he meant to take the ring from her.

"Well, Dr. John Thomas, bishop of Salisbury, was married for the fourth time in 1753, and the wedding ring he gave his wife was engraved with the legend: 'If I survive/ I'll make it five.' "

"How terrible, Peregrine. I hope his wife had it changed."

"I do not know, my sweeting."

Emily blushed at the endearment. How gay and brilliant London now seemed, with the ladies in their thin, fluttering muslins and the stately dandies walking stiffly by in their buckram-wadded coats. She stole a sideways look at the earl. He was wearing a blue morning coat with brass buttons, and, as usual, his cravat was sculptured perfection, and yet he looked at ease in his clothes. She was glad he did not affect the slovenliness of the Corinthians who considered it "quite the tippy" to slouch along looking as much like coachmen as possible.

Few men donned the tricorne these days; most of them wore tall silk hats. Strange to think that only a short time ago, the London haberdasher who designed and wore the first silk hat caused such a commotion that he was charged with a breach of the peace, for it was alleged that the "tall structure, having a shiny lustre, was calculated to frighten timid people." The *St. James's Gazette* reported that several women fainted at the sight, children screamed, dogs yelped, and a small boy broke his arm.

"Where shall we begin?" asked the earl.

Emily all at once did not want to go straight to the dressmaker—this dressmaker whom the earl obviously knew so well. Had he taken his mistress there? "Perhaps we could find some place where I might buy a few feathers for my bonnets," she said. Gypsy bonnets embellished with lots of feathers were all the rage.

"Very well," he said, turning toward Oxford Street. Emily wished he did not have so very great a knowledge of where to buy ladies' apparel.

They went to Nicholay's Fur and Feather Man-
ufactory at 82 Oxford Street. Although Oxford
Street was not as fashionable as Tottenham Court
Road, Nicholay's was considered *the* plumassier.
But even here, his lordship was obviously well
known. A shadow fell on Emily's sunny face.

"In my youth," murmured the earl, waving a
long ostrich plume to and fro and studying Emily's
downcast face, "I was a frequent customer here. I
found it a useful place to buy presents for my lady
relatives."

Emily brightened immediately and bought three
splendid plumes for herself, and three to send home
to Mary. He had, after all, more or less told her she
was the only lady in his life. Emily found herself
looking forward to the visit to the dressmaker.

The dressmaker's rooms were at the top of a
winding flight of stairs in Piccadilly, that fashionable thoroughfare named after the peccadilloes—
those lacy cuffs worn by the cavaliers. Madame
Dupont, the dressmaker, did not betray by even the
flicker of an eyelid that she had seen the earl before. Naturally, a ball gown could not be made, es-
pecially at such short notice, said madame with a
deprecating spread of her long, thin hands, but it
so happened that a certain Lady of Quality had
commissioned a splendid ball gown, but had had to
leave the country before it was delivered.

Emily looked doubtful. She did not like the idea
of buying a dress that had been made for someone
else, but on the other hand, there was no other way
she could get a new ball gown so quickly. Her
doubts fled when Madame Dupont's assistants carried in the gown. It was a slim underdress of blond

silk with an overdress of blond lace. Madame Dupont led her to another room to try it on. It would only need a few pins and tucks to make it a perfect fit. Saying that she would have the gown altered and sent round to the Countess of Devenham's address, Madame Dupont left her assistants to help Emily back into her own clothes.

When Emily quietly entered Madame Dupont's salon some fifteen minutes later, the earl gave her a quick, almost embarrassed look and thrust what looked like a bill into his pocket. Emily's doubts and fears swooped back to plague her again. Madame Dupont would never dream of presenting a bill for the new ball gown so quickly; therefore, it must be some outstanding bill. Whose bill? What woman? Made pettish by anxiety, Emily refused her husband's offer of tea at Gunters, saying she wished to go home and rest before preparing for the ball.

The earl looked at her downcast face and inwardly cursed Cordelia Haddington. How could she be so vulgar as to order gowns from Madame Dupont and then tell the dressmaker to present him with the bills? He longed to say something to Emily to remove the worried, disappointed look from her face, but anything he could think of saying would, he was sure, only make matters worse.

Emily went to bed as soon as they returned home, but she could not sleep. On the one hand she longed to believe her husband was now faithful to her, but a nasty little voice in her brain kept insisting he was lying.

Felice was in good spirits as she helped prepare her mistress for the ball. She had felt Emily's failure to attract her husband reflected badly on the expertise of Lady Devenham's lady's maid. She was almost prepared to forget about the charms of her beloved footman, if only her mistress would take her rightful place in society.

There was a lazy *Miaow* from behind Felice as she heated the curling tongs on the spirit stove. That cat! Felice, like the other servants, was all too aware of my lord's views on Peter. It was unnatural for my lady to dote on the animal so. On the other hand, any further attempt to get rid of the animal would, Felice was sure, result in her instant dismissal. With expert fingers, she teased and arranged Emily's hair into a mass of carefully disarranged curls.

"Felice," said Emily, looking blankly at her own reflection in the mirror. "London is a very wicked place sometimes."

"Indeed, my lady?" said the maid. "It is like other English places, I think."

"No. I have noticed that the gentlemen consider it quite the thing to have . . . to have mistresses."

"La." Felice rolled her eyes. So that was the way of it. She, Felice, had heard of Mrs. Haddington. "That may be, my lady," she said cautiously, "but the gentlemen are fortunate in that no gently-bred English lady would admit to the existence of such a creature."

Emily looked up quickly at the guarded expression on the maid's face and sighed. So even Felice knew. If only she could believe Peregrine—believe that the other woman in his life was now gone forever. There was that bill.

She stood up so that Felice could put her ball

gown over her head and tie the tapes. "We must be quick, my lady," urged Felice. "My lord already awaits you."

Emily looked at the clock. Eight! She had thought they would not leave for at least another hour.

"It is very early, Felice."

"I think my lord he plan to make the other calls."

Emily frowned and bit her lip. That meant, like most of society, the earl had decided to call for ten minutes at several routs and parties before going to the ball. She had hoped to arrive at the ball, fresh, rested, and looking her best. But various jostlings and crushings beforehand would mean arriving fussed, nervous, and already tired. Not guessing that her husband meant to demonstrate to as many members of Polite Society as quickly as possible his good relations with his wife, Emily went downstairs feeling cross and worried and already prepared to find fault with him.

When she saw him waiting for her at the bottom of the stairs, with candlelight shining on the thick waves of his black hair, and when he smiled up at her in a heart-wrenching way, Emily's doubts began to melt. The earl noticed the glow in his wife's eyes and how the beauty of her golden hair was highlighted by the gold of her gown, and he cursed himself for having ignored her for so long.

"Do we have *many* calls to make, Peregrine?" asked Emily. "I had hoped to go directly to the ball, you see."

The earl hesitated. It would be romantic, be wonderful to drive with her through the parks in the old gold light of the setting sun and watch the London sky turn pale green and then purple and look at the ghostly boughs of the apple trees laden down with blossom. On the other hand, he must, for her sake, demonstrate to the polite world that he loved his wife and no other woman.

"It will not take us long to make a few calls," he said, draping her Norfolk shawl over her shoulders.

London had just recovered from an influenza epidemic. The illness or the fear of it had kept the ton at home. Now, with this first glorious spring evening and with the spectre of illness fled from the social scene, the fashionables were out in force. The first rout was a nightmare for country-bred Emily. Where was the joy in dressing up in order to fight one's way up a narrow staircase, to be jostled and pushed and pulled, and then, after ten minutes, to fight one's way back down? The earl's broad shoulders and steadying arm protected Emily from the worst of the buffets, but other ladies screamed and fainted, gentlemen swore and punched, and outside the coachmen came to blows trying to find the best place for their masters' carriage.

After two more such calls, even the earl was forced to notice his pretty wife was beginning to look nervous and jaded. He was used to such affairs himself and used to the company of Cordelia, who, like the rest of society, never rated a rout a success unless one had been nearly crushed to death in the crowd. He smiled ruefully at Emily. "We will go to the ball now, my love. I am sorry I put you to so much discomfort."

Again, Emily's spirits soared. Those two little

words "my love" went straight to her heart, and she smiled at him shyly.

It was wonderful to leave the smells and rumble and jostle of London behind as they rolled past the toll at Hyde Park and then out on the road to Kensington, which was scented with the fresh smell of flowers from all the nurseries on either side.

Kensington nurseries supplied fruit, flowers, and vegetables for the London market, and the only people who did not enjoy the pleasure of the old court suburb were the huntsmen. The Berkeley hounds hunted right up to Kensington Gardens. Lord Alvanley complained that the melon and asparagus beds in the market gardens made the going "devilish heavy . . . up to our hocks in glass all day."

Lord and Lady Foss had moved from town to Kensington, claiming the more salubrious air did wonders for the spleen. They had a very pretty villa not far from Brompton Gardens. As they drew up under the shadow of the portico and Emily heard the thud of feet and the scraping of the fiddles, she found herself hoping there would not be *quite* so many people as there had been at the routs in London.

But as the earl helped her down from the carriage, she could hear more carriages arriving, and the villa already seemed to be full. The ton called themselves The Exclusives and went to great lengths to invent shibboleths and taboos to exclude the mushrooms and Cits. Nonetheless, thought Emily dismally, there seemed to be a horrendous number of people in London society, and all of them, if not already in the villa, were on the point of arrival.

As she went into an anteroom to leave her shawl and repair the damage to her hair, she wished she had brought Felice along. Felice, with her sharp eyes and sharp elbows, would soon have found a place in front of the mirror for my lady. As it was, Emily had to compete with seasoned hands who thrust her aside quite rudely.

Feeling cross, hot, and disheveled, she made only minor adjustments to her appearance by standing on tiptoe and craning her neck to see her reflection in the glass.

The earl did not seem to notice her ruffled manner and appearance as he led her into the ballroom. No sooner had Emily made her curtsy to her host and hostess than a young man came up and begged for the honor of a dance. The earl had already half turned away to talk to someone, so Emily allowed herself to be led away. It was an energetic country dance which went on for at least half an hour. When it was over, she promenaded with her partner. There was no sign of her husband. She was then surrounded by a court of admirers begging for the next dance. Emily was a success. She was vowed the most beautiful woman of the evening. But her success meant nothing to her. All she understood was that all these irritating men with their heavy gallantries were keeping her from the arms of her husband.

The earl had removed himself to the card room after noting his young wife's success. He was very proud of her and, although it hurt to see her dancing with other men, he judged that any lady must be thrilled to be the belle of the ball, and he felt that by leaving her for a short while to enjoy her success, he was in some way making amends for his previous neglect, not realizing that to Emily his present behavior was simply an extension of that very neglect.

Her smile grew more fixed. Her sharp ears began to pick up snatches of gossip, until she became so hypersensitive that she began to wonder whether she was in fact hearing gossip which had never been spoken. "The Countess of Devenham is in looks," a shrill voice said, floating across the musk-laden air. "It is a pity, when one thinks of it . . ." And then the music rose to a crescendo, blotting out the rest of the words.

What is a pity? thought Emily. That he is unfaithful to me?

Her husband appeared suddenly to claim her hand for the next dance. If only it had been the waltz! But it was a lively Scotch reel, which afforded no opportunity for conversation.

Here I am, thought Emily, somewhat hysterically, craving the chance to speak to my own husband. It is ridiculous. And above and below the energetic fiddling came snatches of gossip. "'Tis said that Devenham . . ." ". . . in looks tonight . . . the first time I have seen her . . . never takes her anywhere and of course one knows why. . . ."

And so by the time she found herself promenading on her husband's arm, Emily felt too demoralized to utter a word. The earl looked anxiously at her downcast face and then to where the long windows at the end of the ballroom were open to the calm night. He was just about to suggest they take a stroll in the garden when Lord Brockenham, fat and cheerful, came bouncing up to solicit Emily's hand for the waltz. The earl bowed gracefully and withdrew.

Lord Brockenham was in high alt. He had formed a tendre for Emily and he was glad to see her on such evidently good terms with her husband, for Lord Brockenham delighted in forming hopeless passions. Had Emily liked the vase he had sent? Emily bowed her head and murmured it was beautiful, but unfortunately it had fallen by accident and was now broken. Lord Brockenham vowed cheerfully to "throw" her another.

Dying to lay the latest piece of London gossip at the feet of his adored, Lord Brockenham chattered on. Had Lady Devenham ever heard the on-dit about the Duke of Wellington's marriage? What had happened, Lord Brockenham continued, not waiting for an answer, was that the Iron Duke had received a great shock when he saw Kitty Packenham, the lady who was to become his duchess. She had been pretty Kitty when she rejected his suit in 1793, but her appearance in 1806 when he wed her was another matter. "She has grown ugly, by Jove," the Duke had whispered in the ear of his clergyman brother, Gerald, who was to marry them. "So much for all those endearing young charms," laughed Lord Brockenham. "Not so endearing after all."

"It must have been a very great shock to him," said Emily softly, although she was thinking of her husband. "He must have loved her very much to have waited for her for so long."

"He wasn't in love with her," said Lord Brockenham. "He was talked into it. People said she had waited for *him* and so he felt obliged to marry her."

Was that how Peregrine felt about Mary? Emily wondered. But his welcoming kiss that had been meant for Mary was not that of a cold man who had fallen out of love a long time ago. Oh, dear, perhaps he loved Mary still! Perhaps he had not had a mistress. Perhaps that shadowy woman she had sensed in his life was his longing for Mary. And thus her thoughts went round and round like a fire dog turning the spit.

When the earl at last came to claim her and suggest a walk in the garden, Emily, near to tears, snapped that she was hungry, had had practically no food all day, and did he mean to *starve* her? Looking into her angry, troubled eyes, the earl felt depressed and sad. It was all hopeless. There was no way Emily was going to fall in love with him now. He led her into supper and treated her with aloof courtesy.

Emily thought he would surely notice her misery and at least ask her what was wrong. She did not know that she merely looked sulky, since a young and beautiful face is not made to reflect tragedy.

Out in the ballroom, as if to mock her, the band began to play Thomas Moore's beautiful song written to celebrate the Duke of Wellington's marriage to his Kitty. "Believe Me If All Those Endearing Young Charms" seemed to pound against her ears.

Like Emily, the earl felt so sick and miserable that he thought she might have at least asked him what the matter was. But Emily simply thought he looked bad-tempered and bored.

By the time they were in their carriage and heading homeward, they had both given up any attempt at conversation. The earl was thinking that it was a dismal state of affairs when a man comes home to an empty bed while his young bride sleeps with the cat.

But when they reached their town house, his courage had somewhat returned. Emily looked so beautiful, so fragile in the swaying light of the carriage lamp. He would take her in his arms and kiss her. If she rebuffed him, then that would be the end of that. But at least he could try.

It was like a douche of cold water to find the Ansteys sitting there waiting for them. The earl bowed stiffly and begged to be excused. He muttered something about seeing them at a more respectable hour and took himself upstairs to bed, leaving Emily to comfront them alone.

The Ansteys assumed Emily had heard all the gossip about Cordelia Haddington. Therefore, a bewildered Emily found herself being hugged and kissed and *mourned* over as all the burning, malicious on-dits about Cordelia rose and fell about her ears.

She put up one little hand as if to ward off the clamor. "Enough!" said Mary to Mr. and Mrs. Anstey, noticing her sister's white and stricken face. "I feel we have done a terrible thing. Poor Emily did not know anything of this."

Emily could only nod dumbly.

Then she remembered the earl saying, "There is no other lady in my life . . . now, Emily," and took faint heart, facing Mary proudly and saying, "I did not know the name of the lady. But Peregrine did tell me there had been . . . someone . . . but that there is no longer."

There was a silence. Then Mrs. Anstey began to cry—great, gulping sobs. "Tell her," she wailed.

"Tell me what?" demanded Emily, as rigid as a soldier on parade.

Mr. Anstey sighed heavily. "He was seen driving in the park just the other morning with Cordelia Haddington."

This was true. Cordelia had all but thrown herself under the wheels of the earl's carriage and he had taken her up for a short distance before setting her down outside her house.

"I don't believe it," whispered Emily. But look how ready she had been to believe such a short time ago that Peregrine was in love with Mary.

"I'm afraid it is," said Mr. Anstey. He went on to explain how they had heard all the gossip about the Earl of Devenham and *her* in Malden Grand, and how they had come to town but had waited for information from their scouts before coming to call. "For, mark my words," said Mr. Anstey, "we were not about to believe the first tattletale from town. We had to find out for ourselves."

Weary and defeated, Emily sighed and raised her hand to her bosom.

"Wait for me here," she said in a dull voice. "I will leave with you directly."

Once in her room, Emily rang for Felice and harshly ordered the maid to pack. "You must not tell my lord I am leaving," commanded Emily, looking so stern that Felice decided it would be the best policy to obey. She knew her mistress had never quite forgiven her for throwing the cat out of the inn window. The cat, Peter, yawned and stretched and then began to yowl in protest, as the bandbox with the air holes was produced.

For once, Emily was deaf to his pleas of distress. He was thrust in roughly, and the lid was put securely down. For a while, the large cat kicked and scratched and even succeeded in rolling the box over on its side, but this new hardhearted Emily merely righted the bandbox and told him curtly to be quiet.

Peter's feelings were deeply hurt. He lay in the blackness of the bandbox and sulked.

When at last the packing was finished, Felice realized she was expected to carry the trunks down the stairs without the aid of even a footman, for Emily did not wish to alert her husband. Emily felt she could not bear to look at him again. Felice and Emily finally suceeded in getting all the baggage into the hall, and the Anstey servants carried the bags out to the carriage.

"Did you leave a note?" asked Mary, as the carriage rolled away.

"Why? I have nothing to say to him," said the Countess of Devenham, and turned her face to one side to hide the large tear that was beginning to slide down her cheek.

Chapter Ten

It was no consolation to Emily that the democratic rain which was slowly turning Malden Grand into a swamp was probably ruining the London Season.

To Mary's distress, Emily did not want to talk about her marriage. Apart from asking Mr. Anstey to contact his lawyers and set the annullment in motion, Emily refused to refer to the subject again. She had not wanted to linger in London, although her parents had assured her that the earl did not know the address in Russell Square. She was not afraid he would come looking for her, but she was very much afraid of seeing him again and suffering the resulting pain.

Far better to sit among all the glittery newness of The Elms, listening to the unremitting pitter-patter of the rain, sewing, reading, and talking to one large sulky cat who had not forgiven her for stuffing him in the bandbox.

Outwardly, her life had not changed so very much since the days before her marriage. Often Emily wondered how she had ever managed to bear the monotony of the long days. The worst thing she had had to face on her arrival home was that she loved her husband. The fact that she hated him and felt he had treated her shamefully did not alter that love. Instead of the radiant love Mary felt for her vicar, it was a sad, yearning longing that made the days lie heavy and the nights a torment.

The Ansteys had once more fallen from social grace. No one in the county would believe that Emily had left her husband, for surely one did not leave a rich earl. No, it must be the other way around. The Earl of Devenham had discovered he could not bear to stoop so low. That was the story that Lord and Lady Harrison put about, and they told it so often that they forgot the original spite that had prompted the fiction and came to believe it themselves.

Peter the cat felt his lot was a hard one. His mistress was silent and gloomy and only petted him in an absentminded way. He hated the rain. He hated the tyranny of the servants and the nasty-smelling newness of everything at The Elms.

Then one day the rain stopped and the sun blazed down, warm and golden. Mist rose from the water-logged meadows to be burned off during the day. Lakes dwindled to puddles and the puddles disappeared, leaving everything freshly washed and smiling under the warm rays of the sun.

Peter bided his time. He was not allowed out of doors. Emily felt she had spent too much time cat-chasing. The cat had been trained to perform his necessary functions in a box of gravel.

But the warm days were agony for Emily. Yearning and longing doubled as one golden day led to another. At last, Emily could bear her self-appointed prison no longer and took her book out to the garden and sat under the shade of a large oak. Large white clouds puffed across the blue sky like galleons under full sail, and busy birds pecked for worms on the grass. The French windows of the drawing room stood open.

Peter cautiously stuck his large head around one of the doors. The air smelled sweet. He saw Emily, her fair hair bent over her book. Slinking on his belly, he crept like a shadow across the grass. He reached a gap in the hedge, hesitated, turned his head, and looked back at his mistress. As if aware of the cat's gaze, Emily put down her book and looked up. Peter dived through the gap and ran off down the road.

Emily frowned. Had that been the cat escaping? She picked up her book again, but found the words kept blurring and sliding away. With a little sigh, she arose and went to look for the cat.

Peter played the whole day, chasing birds and hunting voles and field mice. Toward the end of the afternoon, he felt weary with all the unaccustomed exercise and tried to decide whether to find his way home and eat or to lie down and sleep. There was a bridge over the River Axe which skirted the village. It was in full spate, rushing and tumbling over the rocks into the deep pool below the bridge. Peter leaped up onto the parapet. The old stone was warm beneath his paws. He stretched out, full-length, above the rushing river and instantly fell asleep.

His awakening was rude and terrifying. He felt himself seized in a cruel grasp and looked up into the faces of a ring of village boys. "Let's 'ave an 'anging," said one, producing a length of string. This was greeted with cheers, while eyes roamed this way and that, looking for a suitable tree on which to hang the cat.

Mad with terror, Peter bit, clawed, and twisted until one vicious slash caught his captor on the cheek. The boy dropped him, and with a yowl of terror, Peter dived over the parapet and fell like a stone into the pool below.

He surfaced, green eyes bulging with fear, and struck out for dry land. Above him, a jeering voice called, "Let's stone the cat. Let's stone the **** to death!"

Emily sank back into her chair in the garden, feeling depressed and weary. It seemed she could keep nothing she loved, neither husband nor cat. She had searched and searched, but of Peter there had been not the slightest sign.

It was then that she began to cry. She had not cried since that one tear had been shed in the carriage. Now she sobbed and sobbed as if her heart would break. She could not think about her husband's arrogance or his infidelity. She could only remember the charm of his smile and the strength of his body.

Then she heard a carriage on the road. Mary and her parents had left to shop at a nearby town, and Emily felt she could not bear to receive callers. She would hide in her room and when Parsons, the butler, came to fetch her, she would tell him to say she was not at home.

In the cool, dim quiet of her bedroom, where the shutters were closed to keep the sun from fading the carpet, she bathed her face and changed her gown. She was twisting her curls into a knot on top of her head, when Parsons scratched at the door.

"I don't care who it is, Parsons," called Emily. "Tell them I am not at home."

There was a short silence, and then Parsons' voice, muffled, came through the door, "It's his lordship, my lady."

Emily stood very still.

"Your husband, my lady," said Parsons in a louder voice.

Emily took a deep breath. He had come after all. Perhaps he had merely come to arrange a divorce. But she would give herself just one more chance. Surely such a great love could not remain unrequited.

She called, "I will be with his lordship directly," and with trembling hands began to apply a little rouge to her white cheeks.

The Earl of Devenham stood in the hall, his eyes on the stairs. He had come to berate her, to tell her he had had enough of her and her family. It had been the final humiliation to find she had crept from his house like a thief in the night.

Parsons appeared at his elbow to say that cakes and wine had been set out in the drawing room, but the earl snarled, "I will wait here. Leave me alone."

The hall was silent and dim and smelled of paint

and varnish. He heard a light step on the stairs and looked up.

Emily stood on the first landing, looking down at him. She looked thinner. Her dress was of plain white muslin and her golden curls were scraped up on top of her head. Two patches of rouge burned on her white cheeks.

The earl of Devenham thought, all in that moment, that he had never seen such a beautiful sight. His pride fell about him and he held out his arms.

Emily walked slowly down the stairs toward him, hope dawning in her eyes. His arms closed about her and held her close. "Emily," was all he said, but he said it with that strange husky, seductive note in his voice, and she turned her lips up to his.

"My lady!" screamed a small voice behind them.

The earl released Emily and turned around, his eyes blazing with rage. The Ansteys' knife boy stood there with blood running from a cut on his forehead, his jacket dusty and torn.

"What the deuce do you mean by this impertinence?" raged the earl.

"It's the cat!" wailed the boy, staring at Emily and ignoring the earl. "It's in the river and the boys are throwing stones at it. I tried to stop them, but they beat me and kicked me . . ."

And with that, the thoroughly overwrought knife boy sank down onto the hall floor and cried and cried.

The earl took one look at Emily's stricken face, and jerked the boy roughly to his feet. "Look, my lad," he said. "You've behaved like a Trojan so far, and I want you to be brave a little bit longer. Lead us to where you saw the cat."

The boy wiped his streaming eyes with the back of his sleeve, gave a clumsy nod, and set off at a jog trot, with Emily and the earl following close behind.

Peter the cat struggled wearily in the pool. His eyes were beginning to glaze over and he felt the last of his nine lives beginning to slip away. There was a great deal of shouting and commotion on the bank, more than before. He felt himself being seized by the scruff of the neck, and he prepared to die.

The Earl of Devenham, who had cracked two of the village gang leaders' heads together, had dived into the water. He swam to the shore and climbed out and laid the cat on the bank. "Is he dead?" whispered Emily, as if a raised voice would frighten the last of the life out of the cat.

The earl was about to say, "I hope so," but he changed it to, "With any luck, I may be able to get the water out of the brute." He jerked the animal's paws and massaged its stomach until water spurted out of the cat's mouth. Emily stood watching him. The sun filtered down through the trees onto his thick black hair. His fine cambric shirt was molded to his chest. She felt her heart lurch with love.

The cat's chest began to move up and down, and, under the probing of his fingers, the earl felt the beginning of a faint purr.

"He'll live," he said. Emily went to rush into his arms, but stopped short for fear of crushing the cat.

The earl scowled down at the animal in his arms and then began to climb up the rocks to the roadway. Emily climbed after him, while the knife boy, now fully recovered, scampered back to The Elms to be the first to break the news of my lord's routing of the village bullies.

The earl did not speak until he had reached the house. "Where does this creature bed down," he said curtly. "In your room, I suppose?"

Emily nodded miserably. He had looked, that one splendid moment when he had held out his arms, as if he loved her. Now the cat had come between them again. "Better a cat than a mistress," thought Emily with sudden anger.

Housemaids came running with warm towels. Peter was gently rubbed down and placed in his sleeping basket in Emily's room. He felt warm and safe and completely exhausted. He gave a sleepy purr and closed his eyes.

The servants departed, leaving Emily alone in her bedroom with her husband.

Emily looked at him, her eyes guarded, wary. The silence between them lengthened. The light was fading outside and the room was full of shadows.

"Why did you come?" she asked faintly.

He shrugged. She waited for him to say that he had come to arrange a divorce, that he wanted to marry Cordelia Haddington.

He said, "Because I love you with all my heart. I do not even care if you don't want me. I just had to tell you the truth."

"But what about that . . . that woman?" asked Emily.

"Cordelia? I told you that was finished."

"But the day before I left London, you were seen with her in your carriage."

"She practically fell in front of my wheels to stop me. I took her up and took her home. Nothing more."

"But what of that bill that Madame Dupont gave you? You looked embarrassed and thrust it in your pocket when you saw me."

"My life, I confess it was an old bill of Cordelia's. I desperately wanted you to love me. I thought it the wrong time for an explanation."

"I thought you loved her."

"Is that why you left?"

Emily nodded.

He put one knee on his side of her bed. "Come to me," he said huskily.

Emily fell over the bed and tumbled into his arms. "You're wet!" she laughed, feeling his shirt.

"Then undress me."

"I cannot, Peregrine. I am frightened. That has always been the trouble. I am so frightened. I have no experience. I . . ."

His mouth stopped her words and his hands on her body stopped her trembling. He parted her lips and groaned words of love against her mouth, feeling her little hands reach for the buttons of his shirt in the most natural way in the world.

Emily could not remember afterward how they had got out of their clothes. It was almost as if passion had melted them away. A brief spasm of fear stabbed her when she finally lay naked in his arms, but a great red wave of passion came down on her and carried all her fears and inhibitions away.

An hour later, the earl awoke. He felt marvelous. He felt he held the whole world in his arms. Someone—Mary?—was singing out in the garden. "Believe me if all those endearing young charms," she sang in a lilting voice.

The Earl of Devenham felt extremely hungry. He was about to waken his love when he felt movement against his naked back. He lit the rushlight on Emily's side of the bed by stretching over her sleeping figure. Then he turned slowly round.

The cat was stretched out on his other side, purring noisily. It butted its head against his arm.

"No," said the earl softly. "Get out of bed this minute."

And Peter went.